P ○'

Christ

Yes, it is

All our stories this special month involve children at Christmas time, as the adults in their lives try their very best to make the festive season as happy as possible for the little, and not so little, ones concerned, while finding their own special person to love. And sometimes the kids work a little magic of their own, for the best present of all is to become a family.

Our four authors bring you their family traditions from around the world. We visit America with Jessica Matthews, Australia with Meredith Webber, South Africa with Elisabeth Scott and England with Caroline Anderson. The different types of weather in these countries make no difference to the warmth of the Season's Greeting we send to you.

Dear Reader

Christmas is family gathering early in the day for The Present Opening. Children allowed to open one present while they wait for late arrivals—'No, twenty-two is too old to qualify!' Then giving and receiving, bright paper flying, shouts of excitement and pleasure—'Just what I wanted!' Fingers brush across soft lingerie, linger on the covers of new books—'Can't wait until everyone's gone and I can begin to read. . .!'

And Christmas lunch—sweet scent of frangipani flowers scattered on the table. We break our bon-bons, read weak jokes, don our party hats and tuck in to roast turkey, ham and piles of baked vegetables. We've tried having it on Christmas Eve, tried cold lunches—prawns and crab and luscious tropical fruit—but it's not the same. Even in our soaring summer heat, we come back to the traditions of a heritage acknowledged most strongly on this one day of the year.

Happy Christmas!

Meredith Webber

A FATHER
FOR CHRISTMAS

BY
MEREDITH WEBBER

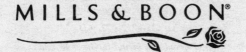

MILLS & BOON®

*First published in Great Britain 1997
Harlequin Mills & Boon Limited,
Eton House, 18-24 Paradise Road, Richmond, Surrey TW9 1SR*

© Meredith Webber 1997

ISBN 0 263 80516 6

*Set in Times 10 on 12 pt. by
Rowland Phototypesetting Limited
Bury St Edmunds, Suffolk*

03-9712-47229-D

*Printed and bound in Great Britain
by Mackays of Chatham PLC, Chatham*

CHAPTER ONE

PEACE!

Richard listened to the silence. The last faint rumble of the removal van had died away and, apart from the odd mutter of an unidentified bird and the splash of the creek which he knew ran through the bottom of the property, there was no sound.

He threaded his way through the maze of packing cases and walked out onto a wide timber deck. The air was sweet, untainted by city dust and diesel fumes, and the sky a richer blue than he could ever have imagined. Below the deck was a grassy swale, lush and smooth, and beyond that the land dipped towards the rich green band of trees and shrubs that hid the creek from view.

His creek!

Sucking in the air greedily, he forgot the multitude of doubts he'd been experiencing in the exhausting chaos of relocation. He'd told his agent to find him a haven of peace and solitude for the Christmas break and she'd come up trumps again! She'd even had the lawn mown, by the look of things. He should fax her straight away to thank her—

The blast of rock music was so loud, so close, that it struck him like a physical assault. He strode in the direction of the sound—towards the southern end of the deck—resisting an impulse to clap his hands over his ears, then stared, bemused, at his lower terrace. The source of the noise was a long, black cassette player of some kind. A ghetto-blaster? He'd seen advertisements for similar instruments of torture.

It was set on the low brick wall that edged the terrace, and four children were lined up in front of it, gyrating to the noise.

'Hey!' he yelled, but the human larynx was no match for modern technology.

Anger erupted like a scalding geyser. He took the shallow steps two at a time, swept across the terrace and slapped his hand on the infuriating machine, pushing at buttons and slides until the noise ceased.

'What do you think you're doing,' he demanded, turning towards the four miscreants, 'making that unholy racket on my property? Get out of here, the lot of you! Get out—now!'

He could hear his voice roaring in his ears and knew it was because the last few weeks had been mentally and physically exhausting. Camels' backs and last straws came to mind, as there'd been four years of increasing pressure before that.

Not that his roaring was affecting the trespassers. The tallest, a boy who could have been anything from ten to thirteen, moved closer to his sister and slipped his arm around her shoulder, drawing her protectively close. The other two, a boy and a girl, both redheads and alike enough in size and colouring to be twins, had also drawn closer to each other. They were wary but not afraid, he guessed, seeing the wide brown eyes darting from him to the older pair, then back to him again.

'We didn't know you were here—that anyone was here. The place has been empty for months and months now.'

The older boy spoke, standing up very straight and

meeting Richard's fury with a strangely adult blend of apology and composure.

'Which still gives you no right to trespass!' Richard fumed. The child's attitude disconcerted him and the way the older girl was cringing behind her brother made him even more furious. What did she think he was? A child-molester? His anger escalated.

'Go on, take your wretched noise machine and get out of here, and be glad I haven't reported you to the police!'

'But Kyle keeps the—' The younger boy started to speak but his brother stopped him with a quick movement of his hand.

'Hush, Mikey! The man's right. We shouldn't have been here.'

'But we can't practise at home with Marnie sleeping,' the younger girl wailed. 'We'll never get it right in time.'

'We'll go down to the creek and practise there,' the boy told her. 'Now, take Jill and Mikey and go on home.'

Richard frowned. His anger was fading and the exhaustion that had forced him to seek this seclusion was creeping back through his bones. The elder boy still stood his ground and, as the three younger children disappeared into a clump of bushes on the boundary of his property, Richard was reminded of an army sergeant masterminding a retreat. Get the troops safely out of the way first, then either fight or run yourself.

Which option would the boy choose?

'I'm sorry we disturbed you, sir, but we've done no harm here,' he said.

An apology that wasn't an apology, Richard realised, but he was too tired to do more than wave his hand towards the cassette player before he turned and walked away.

From the deck he could see the roof of a house on the neighbouring property, and assumed the children must live there. Jackie had mentioned neighbours.

'Not so close you'd actually hear them,' she'd assured him, and he'd agreed with her that, in time, he might appreciate having someone to wave to occasionally.

But children? And four of them?

Children!

He groaned as he remembered something else Jackie had mentioned—something about an appeal for the Abused Children's Trust on Christmas Day. He'd said no, but she'd never take one no as a final answer!

He was still scowling when he heard the music start up again. It was dimmed by distance and diluted by the thick scrub along the creek, but the thumping base rhythm carried clearly enough to chase him into the house.

The packing cases littering the floor seemed to have multiplied in his absence, and he knew he didn't have the energy to move again. He shrugged, sighed and began to unpack. Once order was restored he'd feel better. An orderly house promoted inner peace.

That sounded good. Had he read it somewhere or written it himself?

The thought depressed him. Would he ever regain the ease with which the words had flowed when he'd written his first book? Was 'writing' really what he wanted to do? Wasn't it distancing him from the profession he'd chosen because he enjoyed kids' company—and because he had once fancied he had something to offer in the field?

He heard an echo of his voice as he'd roared at the young intruders, and wondered if he'd lost touch with those beginnings—lost the special magic that grew out of associating closely with children.

He shrugged again, mentally admitting how badly he needed this break.

'And he yelled at us!' Margaret emphasised. 'Yelled and yelled and talked about calling the police. Kyle explained we didn't know he'd shifted in, but he was still cross as two sticks.'

Marnie continued dishing up the dinner, her lips twitching at Margaret's expression. She not only looked like a miniature version of her grandmother, but she had absorbed enough of Marnie's mother's sayings to sound like a tape-recording of the older woman at times.

'Perhaps we could bake him a cake and take it over after dinner to welcome him and his family,' Marnie suggested.

She was dividing up the meat loaf and thinking about Petunia Crosby, who was becoming more and more irrational as her confinement grew closer, so when Kyle said, 'I wouldn't bother welcoming *him*!' in a stern voice, she had to pause for a moment to work out who 'him' was.

'No cake?'

She grinned at Kyle, considering how much she depended on the scrawny, dark-haired boy. He'd been undernourished for so long that he was small for his fifteen years, but in his head he was going on fifty and she had learned to respect his judgements.

'I wouldn't waste the ingredients,' he said. 'He looked like one half of a DINK.'

'Dink? What's a dink? You know I can't keep up with teenage slang. I stalled back when "cool" became "filthy".'

The three younger children turned to Kyle, and Marnie realised how much they, too, relied on him. They were watching him as ancient Greeks must have watched the Oracle at Delphi. They were about to learn something new!

'It's not slang,' he protested, and the children lost interest. 'Well, not our slang. It's in the papers all the time—you know—couples without kids. It stands for. . .' he hesitated, as if determined to get it right '. . . Double Income No Kids—D-I-N-K—see?'

'Ah!' Marnie said, as the picture became clearer. 'I thought they were yuppies.'

She loved these conversations with Kyle, loved to see the pride swell inside him as he 'explained' things to her. '*Give kids credit for what they know*,' her child-rearing bible told her. '*Let them tell* you *things*.'

'Same kind of people but yuppies can have kids,' Kyle assured her, and she nodded as if she finally understood.

'Well, if they haven't any kids maybe I won't bake a cake, but I should pop over and welcome them some time soon.'

She sat down and began to eat, knowing the children would never begin without her. Perhaps Kyle was wrong about the man—perhaps he'd been tired after the move and had vented his anger without thinking. As she made the mental excuses she recognised her own disappointment.

When the 'For Sale or Lease' sign had disappeared from the property next door she'd begun to picture her new neighbours. A family with kids who'd play with her kids—perhaps a woman who would become a friend. She hadn't thought about this woman's husband—these imaginary children's father—at all. The men in her life were useful for babysitting but apart from that, she rarely considered men as a species these days.

'My turn to clear away,' Mikey announced. They'd all finished eating while she'd been lost in her dream of delightful new neighbours. Too bad it wasn't to be.

'OK, set to,' she told him, then turned to Kyle and Jill. 'Homework, you two. How's the project going, Jill?'

The beautiful grey eyes turned towards her and she felt a now-familiar stab of pain. Then Jill smiled and nodded and Marnie reminded herself how far they'd come already in rehabilitating the injured child who dwelt within Jill's skin.

'Good girl!' she said, as if the smile and nod had been an exposition of great length. 'Let me know when you're ready for me to look at it.'

She gave another nod, then followed Kyle out of the room.

'Jill dances best of all of us,' Margaret told her, dragging a little stool across to the sink so that she could dry the dishes as Marnie washed them. 'Sometimes Kyle puts on your fairy music and she dances to that by herself. It's like she was born to be a fairy.'

Marnie knelt down and hugged the little girl.

'Maybe music and dancing will help her get better,' she whispered, pressing her face into the red curls and sniffing at the baby smell that still clung to them. She felt a rush of affection for her little family and sighed with the sheer joy of it all. Who needed friendly neighbours?

She was reading the twins a bedtime story when Matt Crosby phoned. Petunia's waters had broken and she was panicking, Could Marnie come?

'You know what to do?' she asked Matt, and listened while he repeated the instructions she'd left pinned on the wall above the telephone. There was a second list pinned in the downstairs playroom where Petunia had decided she wanted to give birth. Marnie had reservations about the underwater birth, but she'd attended one at a private hospital and had read all the literature she could find in case Petunia insisted on it.

As Matt finished his recitation she wondered again why someone as sensible as Matt would choose a scatter-brained wife like Petunia.

'I'll be there as soon as I can,' she assured him, and hung up. She checked the list hung above her phone— more a timetable than a list, really—and dialled Jim's number.

'I'm called out and it could be an all-nighter—do you mind?' she asked.

He never did and she said a silent prayer of thanks that he had such an understanding wife.

'Tell the kids I'll be with them by nine,' he told her. 'What's the latest with Mikey? Is he back on wheat products?'

'Yes, but fruit on his breakfast cereal,' she reminded him. 'No sugar or honey.'

'Poor little bugger,' Jim muttered, and before Marnie could argue he added, 'I know, I know! Gareth Gordon, the great god and guru, says—'

Marnie chuckled as she said goodbye. It was all right for Jim to tease her, but when she'd been landed with the twins she'd known so little about rearing children. As a midwife, her experience of babies ended with their safe delivery—well, by the time they were twelve months old, anyway. She'd babysat the twins, but putting them to bed and reading them a story was very different from a twenty-four-hour-a-day type of responsibility. The first thing she'd done had been to rush out and buy a 'bringing up baby' book by the noted paediatrician Dr Gareth Gordon.

She now had four of Dr Gordon's books, ranging from the original purchase to his latest, *Trials, Tears and Teenagers*, and also had the paper delivered by the mailman on Thursdays so she could read his syndicated column. With Dr Gordon's help, she was going to be the best mother in the world.

She wrote the Crosbys' number clearly on the whiteboard by the phone—'*Establish a whiteboard message centre early in your children's lives*,' Dr Gordon had told her in book three. Now all the family wrote each other messages, although Mikey and Margaret still drew pictures that showed her they were at the creek or the climbing tree or Mr Brown-across-the-creek's dairy.

She checked the contents of her bag, then went back to kiss the twins goodnight.

'Baby coming?' Mikey asked, and she nodded, pleased at how well they accepted her absences. Surely that meant they were secure, she thought as she walked through to tell Jill and then Kyle where she was going.

'Who's doing the night shift?' Kyle asked.

'Jim,' she told him. 'He'll be here before you go to bed. Crosbys' number is by the phone and don't forget we have a neighbour now in a real emergency.'

'I'm sure he'd be delighted to come to our rescue— not!' Kyle muttered. She grinned at his scornful expression.

'Do you mind being left with the kids like this?' she asked. 'Do you ever resent having to take over until someone else gets here?'

She didn't know why she asked but, as she saw a flush of colour darken his tanned cheeks, she was glad she had. Maybe she took his compliance too much for granted.

'Of course I don't,' he muttered at her. 'Least I can do.'

She crossed the room in two strides and wrapped her arms around his shoulders.

'You owe me nothing,' she scolded. 'Please don't ever feel beholden. Don't think you have to stay here with the kids and me as some kind of repayment.'

He nuzzled his head against her shoulder, and she smelt the boy-man smell of him, so different from Margaret's baby-smell.

'Guess we're stuck with each other until I finish school!' he mumbled, and her heart clenched with happiness. It was only in the last two months that Kyle had actually talked about the future. Up until then he'd acted like a guest—passing through on his way to somewhere else—intent on staying only long enough to help Jill settle in.

Marnie knew it was his fear of being hurt again that made him hesitate to put down roots, and she'd prayed he'd find the courage to try to stick it out. But it had to be his choice, as she'd told him from the beginning.

Now it seemed as if the choice might have been made.

'I'd better go,' she told him, and dropped a light kiss on his thick thatch of hair before she released him. 'Remind Jim to leave the hall light on, won't you?'

'He knows that!' Kyle told her. 'You get going or the flower-lady will have the kid without you.'

Marnie smiled at him and left, heading outside to where her battered old Volvo station wagon was parked beneath an arch of bougainvillea. She backed out, spun around and then headed up the drive. Above her and to the right she saw a light on in the upstairs bedroom of the house next door.

She'd have to call in and say hello some other time, she realised, and wondered how her new neighbours were coping with their unpacking.

Richard was stacking books on the pine bookshelves he'd set up beside his desk when the headlights drew his attention to the house next door. He glanced at his watch. Eight-thirty. Surely a bit late for the children's parents to be going out for dinner? Was the young boy old enough to babysit?

He remembered someone asking him at what age a teenager could take over responsibility for younger siblings, and he'd hesitated, not wanting to give a definite answer because responsibility meant so many things. The questioner had left the book-store dissatisfied with him and he'd felt inadequate and annoyed with himself. It had been another indication that he had to step off the merry-go-round before he was whirled into some kind of frenetic oblivion.

He was still gazing idly out the window when new headlights lit the darkness. The parents returning? He peered out and realised that it was a smaller car coasting slowly down the slope towards the house. Pleased to have something to divert him from his unpacking, he watched it stop, then saw a man emerge from it and stride towards the house.

Maybe a lover calling after the husband's driven away, he told himself and smiled. And maybe he'd give up non-fiction and start writing sex and sizzle!

He turned from the window, wondering if perhaps he should have chosen the other upstairs room for his study. Would this view of the neighbours' drive and front door divert him from his work? Would he be drawn into fantasies about their lives, making their presence another excuse not to write?

He'd made the other room his bedroom, thinking he'd be further from the neighbours if the children played their loud music early in the morning when he was trying to sleep. He was a night-person, doing his best work while the rest of the world was sleeping, but he needed to sleep in in the mornings or his brain wouldn't function next night.

He sighed and looked beyond the house next door to the dark folds of the mountains and the star-encrusted night sky above them. He breathed deeply, again savouring the special purity of the untainted air. From somewhere in the valley beyond the creek came the mournful bellow of a cow. Was she calling to her calf? Parental responsibility, that's what he was tackling this time—parents and partners.

Could he draw parallels between human and animal behaviour to give his work a fresh approach? He forgot his neighbours and the twinkling light-show of the stars and sat down at his desk, scribbling notes to himself on a piece of discarded packing paper.

Marnie threaded her fingers into her hair and massaged her scalp. She was getting too old to go without sleep.

'I think I'd like to go back into the bath,' Petunia moaned, and Marnie clenched her teeth. Petunia had been in and out of the bath fourteen times, and each time Marnie and Matt had had to take more of the woman's weight as she clambered in and out of the hot tub. Marnie judged she was in transition—the second stage about to begin—and Petunia still hadn't quite decided if she was going to give birth in or out of the tub.

'The head's engaged and you're fully dilated,' she warned Petunia, 'so don't go back in unless that's where you want to be when the baby arrives.'

Her own uneasiness was escalating with her tiredness. Remember to keep a finger on the cord, she reminded herself as they heaved Petunia up the steps and settled her back in the water. While it's pulsing the child doesn't need to breathe.

'I need to push,' Petunia told them. 'No, I don't want to do it in the water. I want to squat!'

Marnie hid her exasperation and reached out to help Matt, who was standing in the tub behind his wife and supporting her under the armpits. Once she was out Matt dried her, while Marnie spread clean towels over the soft rubber mat she'd already placed on the floor.

'Why squatting?' Matt asked, as even his patience with his labouring wife began to wear thin. 'Marnie can't see what's happening.'

'It's a natural position,' Marnie assured him. 'A lot of women prefer it these days. In many ways it makes sense as it helps the sacral area to move more easily, pulling back the pelvic floor and allowing the baby to slide through.'

Matt nodded as he helped Petunia into a comfortable position, then he knelt behind her and rubbed her back. Marnie could see little of what was going on but her hands knew their job, and she felt the head emerge. Her fingers checked to see that the cord wasn't wrapped around the infant's neck, then felt the twist as the baby turned to ease its shoulder past the pelvis.

Maybe the warm water had helped the perineum expand, she thought as the infant emerged easily into her hands.

'You've done it, love!' she heard Matt cry as she

lifted the tiny form, wiped its face and watched it turn a satisfactory pink. She handed the baby girl to Petunia, who lay back against her husband and held the infant to her breast.

Marnie grabbed a big foam wedge she carried with her and used it and pillows to prop Petunia in a half-reclining position on the floor. She and Petunia had argued about using a drug to hasten the final stage of labour, and she couldn't remember Petunia's final decision.

'I don't think so,' Matt whispered as if he sensed her dilemma.

She glanced at Petunia, happily cooing at her new daughter, and put away the tiny vial she'd had ready on the table. It meant she'd have to stay a little longer to make sure there was no excessive bleeding and check back on Petunia later in the day, but she was becoming more and more interested in drug-free births and was following up on the children she'd delivered this way.

Remembering the prolonged agony of the twins' drug-supported arrival into the world, she wondered if it might have contributed to Mikey's allergy problems.

No doubt aided by the baby's suckling, the placenta was delivered quickly. Marnie retrieved it, clamped the cord and then held it for Matt to cut. She saw the tears glitter in his eyes and felt her own silly rush of emotion. You're a midwife—you should be used to it, she reminded herself.

'Do you want a bath or straight to bed?' she asked.

'A quick bath then bed, I think, for all three of us,' Petunia said, and Marnie knew it was nearly time for her to go. She could share the pain and joy of childbirth but she was still an outsider—not part of that magical inner circle of mother, father, child.

She took the baby, weighed and measured her, then bathed and wrapped her warmly. Matt and Petunia would dress her later when they'd had time to examine the minute perfection of the little one. She tucked the baby into the prepared crib and busied herself tidying up while Matt bathed his wife then helped her tenderly out of the tub. He wiped her down with warm dry towels, then slid a crisp white nightdress over her head. She might have been a princess, not the dithery, often-cranky, always nagging, slightly overweight woman he'd known since he was six.

Once dressed and ready, Petunia picked up her child, thanked Marnie in a cursory fashion, ordered a cup of tea and baked beans on toast from her bemused husband and made her regal way upstairs to bed.

She *knew* she was a princess, Marnie realised—if only for a night!

She cleaned up the mess, threw the wet towels into the washing machine and set it going and packed her bag. Outside a slight lightening of the sky heralded the day. She called goodbye to Matt and left, starting the car and driving away as quietly as possible—as if a roaring engine might awaken the shadows by the side of the road.

Another night, another baby! She'd had three busy months and was blaming the baby boom on the previous Christmas season and the renewed hope a new year always generated. Dr Gordon should do a study on the number of babies born in particular months and take it back forty weeks to guess at possible causes!

She grinned to herself. Such silly thoughts were the product of too little sleep, she reminded herself.

As she turned into her drive and cut the engine she

noticed a light on next door. Maybe Kyle was wrong and they did have a child. She hoped it wasn't ill.

Richard was still at his desk, but had found a notebook for the sudden outpouring of ideas, and was still writing when the noise of a car engine reverberated through the stillness. Peering blearily through the window, he realised it must be close to dawn for the land had lost the thick darkness of the night and he could distinguish the shapes of trees.

The car turned into his neighbour's drive, then the engine was cut and it slid noiselessly down the hill to disappear into what appeared to be an overgrown carport at the side of the house. The other car was still parked outside the front door.

So they're a two-car family, Richard thought, although he wasn't particularly interested in his neighbours. Have to have two cars when they're this far out of town, he decided, as a woman appeared, walking into the circle of light thrown by the lamp above the front door.

The first thing he noticed was her hair—a fiery blaze of red in the greyness of the dawn.

Then her legs!

He leaned closer to the window, uneasily aware of voyeurism—but most women he knew didn't peel off their skirt on the way from the car to the front door. He watched, riveted, as she slung the skirt over her shoulder, then began to unbutton her shirt. Was she so eager to get into bed? Did the mere thought of her husband excite her so much that she was naked by the time she hit the bedroom door?

He saw her ease her shirt off one shoulder and thought he detected a tiredness in her movements. Maybe she worked nights at the butter factory in town. With four kids, she was probably more interested in sleep than sex, he decided.

He sat down and wrote another note.

CHAPTER TWO

'THAT man yelled at us again, and he chased Mikey and Jill!'

Marnie sat up in bed, trying to clear the sleep-induced fluff from her brain so she could think.

'What man?' she asked, drawing the little girl into her arms and holding her close.

'The man next door,' Margaret sobbed, smearing tears across Marnie's bare shoulder.

She kissed the child and hugged her tight, then sat her on the bed while she struggled out of it. She'd lain down for ten minutes' rest, and shouldn't have gone to sleep—not with Kyle playing soccer after school and no one here to keep an eye on the younger children.

'Where's Mikey now?' she asked, knowing the little scamp should be her first concern. She pulled a pair of shorts on over her panties, then tied a halter top around her neck and fastened it at the back.

'He's in Mr Brown's paddock, him and Jill. They were on the bridge when the man yelled so they went that way and I ran back here.'

The sobs had subsided into occasional hiccups and Marnie guessed that Margaret was quite enjoying the drama of the situation.

'Well, we'd better go and rescue them, I suppose.'

She pushed her feet into a pair of leather sandals and set out, angry with herself for neglecting the children but even more annoyed with a neighbour who kept harassing her brood. She'd tell him a thing or two!

'He's coming up the hill,' Margaret muttered at her as they crossed the side lawn towards the boundary hedge. She peered through the tangle of plumbago bushes that separated the two properties and glimpsed a figure striding up the slope.

'The tunnel's this way!' Margaret tugged at her hand, leading her towards the low, cave-like entrance which children of another generation had carved through the straggly undergrowth.

Did she really want to crawl through there and confront her neighbour? Wouldn't she be better walking back up to the road and making a more dignified entrance down his front drive?

'Go on!' Margaret urged, giving her a little push.

'*Always act immediately.*' She reminded herself of Dr Gordon's words, visualising his triangular diagram of how tension could escalate between parents and children proportionally to the time wasted between the transgression and the confrontation. Assuming that the same would apply with neighbours, she bent double and pushed her way into the tunnel.

He had passed her by the time she emerged so she had to call to him.

'Excuse me!' The words stumbled off her tongue as her first clear glimpse revealed a man of remarkable size—tall and broad-shouldered, narrow-hipped, suntanned legs. . .

'Not another one!' the man muttered, turning to survey her with the kind of distaste she felt for cockroaches.

The words stiffened her resolve but she had to fight an impulse to lift her hands to her hair and pull out all the bits of twig and leaf she was certain had accumulated there. Front on, he was impressive.

'I want to speak to you about the children,' she said firmly.

'Oh, yes?' he sneered, and his gaze skated from the top of her head to the tips of her sandals, then tracked back up to settle on her rapidly colouring face. 'And who are you? Big sister or the nanny?'

Anger she usually reserved for stupidity began to stir to life, and Marnie drew herself up to her full five feet six and glared at him.

'I'm their mother!' she stated clearly, and enjoyed the flicker of surprise in his eyes. They were grey—not unlike Jill's—

Thinking of Jill fuelled her anger but she held it in check.

'And I'd like to point out that yelling at children is counter-productive.' The man seemed taken aback so she continued with one of her favourite 'Dr Gordon' arguments. 'Children hear the anger, not the words,' she explained. 'The anger blocks their minds with either fear or confusion—they don't hear what you're saying, only the tone of your voice.'

'Fear!' her neighbour snorted. 'Those young hellions were dancing on the logs across the creek. They obviously don't know the meaning of the word "fear" and no one's warned them of the consequences of a fall— concussion, broken limbs—'

'Drowning!' Marnie offered helpfully. 'Or all of the above!' She shrugged, then explained, 'The water in that part of the creek is deep enough to cushion a fall and the logs aren't high enough for them to be hurt hitting it.'

She was about to point out that they'd been dancing across the logs for nearly a year now with no mishaps, but something about this man was making her uneasy.

Was it the way he was looking at her? That mixture of disapproval and surprise in his eyes?

'It's our bridge across to Farmer Brown's!' The little voice was unexpected, but it was full of fighting spirit!

Margaret's fingers slid into Marnie's hand and she was pleased the child had had the courage to follow her through the tunnel and stand up to this...this tyrant!

'They cross the creek on the logs all the time,' Marnie told him, tilting her own chin as she tried to match Margaret's defiance. 'And balancing like that is good for them developmentally.'

She didn't know why she was telling him that, unless repeating his words gave her a feeling that her beloved Dr Gordon was with her, backing her up in this argument with a stranger. 'And I don't think they'd ever fall unless someone frightens the wits out of them by yelling— which, as I was telling you, is something you should never do with children.'

She let the words come out in a rush for the man was frowning quite fearsomely and she sensed that he was about to storm away.

And she didn't want him to!

'The logs are on my property!'

She dragged her thoughts back.

'But the best swimming hole is on ours. You're in the country now,' she explained, 'and we're neighbours. Neighbours share! Generations of people have crossed the creek on those logs, just as they've swum in our water-hole in summer. The creek belongs to all of us.'

His frown deepened into a scowl.

'Not my part of it!' he growled, but Marnie had been diverted by the sight of two small patches of red flitting through the bushes along the side of the creek. Jill and

Mikey had re-crossed the bridge while she kept the ogre at bay!

'Just like the Three Billy Goats Gruff!' She smiled at the aptness of the analogy.

'What did you say?' the man roared, and Margaret's fingers tightened on hers.

'I'm sorry, I was thinking aloud,' she muttered. She did that far too often when she was alone—it must stop. 'And you're yelling again. It's not good for Margaret to see an adult losing control.'

He glowered at her and in the dark fury of his face, she could almost read the things he'd have liked to say. It was a pity, she decided, because he'd have a handsome face if he stopped being angry. It had good clean lines— a sculpted look which was more usual in people who were underweight or malnourished. Not that there was anything underweight or malnourished about the rest of his body—

'Get off my property!' he said, spacing out the words so she could have no doubt that he meant what he said. She dragged her mind away from his physical attributes.

This was a man at the extreme limit of his control she realised, but she couldn't resist having the last word.

She smiled at him and tilted her head to one side.

'Well, now that you've asked so nicely, I guess Margaret and I could go,' she said sweetly, then she turned away and sauntered casually back towards the tunnel.

Her dignified exit was slightly marred by having to bend over double to follow Margaret through the narrow opening but, on the whole, she felt she hadn't done too badly.

Richard felt his anger fading as he watched the slim white legs pick their way across his grass. She'd burst from the bushes like a creature of the forest, a tendril of pale-leafed vine tangling through the dark red rich abundance of her hair. Then she'd had the hide to quote his own words at him and the frustrated anger, never far below the surface of his outward control these days, had exploded.

He watched her bend, saw her neat buttocks tighten the denim of her very brief shorts and wondered if heading to the bush had been such a good idea after all. At least in the city there were any number of women he could call up when he felt like female company. He would never have been reduced to lusting after a married woman with four children. Not that he was, of course!

He studied the bushes, wondering whether he should build a fence, and glimpsed a flash of red on the far side. Two flashes of red. The devils dancing on the logs had both been wearing red shirts! They'd crept back across the creek while their mother had him baled up on the slope—and she'd known it, the red-haired witch!

Billy Goats Gruff indeed! he thought and chuckled, surprising himself with the unfamiliar sound of his own laughter.

Kyle was coming down the drive as they walked back to the house, and Mikey ran to tell him of their most recent encounter with the new neighbour while Margaret told Jill how brave she'd been. Marnie heard the words but wasn't listening, too busy analysing why an arrangement of features on one face could look ordinary yet the same arrangement on another could make her heart rate rise.

Not that it had risen much! Just tripped a trifle. Perhaps it was because his eyes were like Jill's, and his thick brown hair, flopping forward onto his forehead on one side, reminded her of Kyle.

And she wouldn't think about his lips, she told herself, herding the girls towards the house. It was no good thinking about lips, no matter how shapely and clearly defined they might be. Thinking of lips led to thinking of kisses and there was absolutely no point in letting her thoughts stray *that* far.

'Everything OK with the ogre?' Kyle asked as their paths converged.

Marnie grinned at him and nodded.

'Everything's fine!' she assured him, and asked about soccer practice.

He'd been new to the game when he'd started at the high school in Clareville, but his size, speed and judgement had made him a natural on the wing and the school's team was leading the district competition.

'Practice went well. Did you get some sleep?' He was studying her, and she knew he always worried when she'd missed a night's sleep. She nodded her reassurance and reached out to ruffle his hair, touched by his concern.

'About half an hour between afternoon tea and when the grumpy old curmudgeon next door started raising hell again,' she told him. 'I had an antenatal clinic this morning, then went back to see Petunia and the baby after lunch. She wants to call her Sunshine, but I think Matt's putting his foot down about it.'

Kyle chortled with glee. His favourite joke was that Petunia had changed her name by deed poll, and when asked what it had been originally he came up with Daffodil, or Agapanthus, or some equally unlikely suggestion.

Marnie laughed with him, pleased they could share a joke.

Just another day, she realised, as she directed the
rituals of bathtime, dinner and homework.

So why did she feel dissatisfied?

Richard sat at his desk and watched the lights go out in
the house next door. What was it about the place that
drew his attention and disrupted his concentration? He
remembered the little girl creeping quietly across the
grass until she could reach out and grasp her mother's
hand. Somehow the image had stuck in his mind—along
with pert denim-clad buttocks—and blocked his thought
processes.

Was it the idea of 'family' that the image conjured
up? Heavens, he'd written about families for years without ever feeling the slightest urge to have one of his
own so why should that be unsettling? In fact, he'd seen
so many families in his studies he'd resigned himself to
a single life. Some families worked and people like him
did all they could to help them remain as a cohesive
unit, but so many of them disintegrated that he'd decided
long ago he'd just as soon not take the risk.

A new square of light appeared and, as a slim shadow
crossed the window, he realised he must be looking
down on his neighbour's bedroom. In the silence of the
night he heard the protesting screech of a sash window
being raised and he drew back so he could see without
being seen.

She was framed in the oblong of light, wearing what
looked like an over-sized T-shirt, and as he watched she
lifted up her arms and threw back her head, as if to drink
her fill of the magic of the night air.

Then she half turned and he fancied she had glanced
towards his house—towards the window where he
hovered in the shadows.

This is ridiculous behaviour, he told himself, and decided to shift his study to the other upstairs room first thing in the morning. He went downstairs to make a cup of coffee. By the time he returned to his desk, the light was gone from that window, and only a dim glow showed a light left on somewhere in the house.

'*Don't ignore the fears of childhood*,' he'd once written. '*If children are afraid of the dark leave a light on in a hall so they can see the familiar shapes of furniture.*'

Had his neighbour read all his books, or just the one she'd quoted at him?

The thought reminded him of the book he was supposed to be writing now—and the deadline he'd promised to meet. Wasn't that why he'd hidden himself away in the bush for the Christmas break—why he'd had Jackie find him this retreat?

He read through the notes he'd made the previous evening and realised he'd been carried too far from his theme. Some of the ideas would be useful, but he had to nail the beginning.

'Parents and partners,' he wrote for the one-thousandth time, as if his projected title might conjure up the ideas he needed. But as he sipped at his coffee, he was wondering about the redhead's partner, and trying to work out how old she was. At least thirty, judging by the older lad, yet she didn't look that old. . .

'PARENTS AND PARTNERS!'

He scrawled the words in block letters across a page. He *had* to get back to work or the whole exhausting exercise of shifting would prove worthless. He didn't believe in writer's block, he reminded himself, then he threw his pen down on the desk, switched off his light and headed for bed. Maybe he'd try writing in the morning for a change. Maybe that would work.

Maybe!

It didn't work so he tackled the rest of his unpacking, working through the day to put some order into his surroundings. He was arranging his meagre supply of crockery in the kitchen cupboards when the small boy appeared on the deck.

He looked hot and flustered and Richard suspected that the grubby marks on his cheeks might be tears, hastily scrubbed away as signs of weakness.

'Can you come quickly?' he asked rushing through the open glass doors. 'It's Gran! She fell down and is lying on the floor and we can't make her wake up.'

He seized Richard's hand and dragged him towards the door.

'Kyle comes home late today and Marnie had a call-out, but she always said in any emergency. . .' he stumbled over the word but his feet were sure as he hurried Richard towards the small hole in the bushes '. . .get an adult.'

He indicated to Richard to duck and led him into the tunnel.

All right for kids and slim young women, Richard thought as he hunkered down and crawled along the well-worn track. Twigs reached out to grab at his clothes and tear at his skin, but his own sense of urgency kept him moving as quickly as he could manage.

'Jill dialled Emergency and asked for an ambulance,' the child added, then raced across the lawn towards the house.

Richard followed him, hurrying through a wide entry to where the two girls knelt beside a middle-aged woman. Open cupboard doors and an overturned stool told the story more clearly than words. He was glad the children had called an ambulance as the woman's arm lay at an unnatural angle. She must have flung it out to save herself and landed awkwardly on it.

She stirred as he took her pulse, and her eyelids lifted to reveal the golden brown eyes inherited by her daughter and the twins.

'Stupid woman, aren't I?' she muttered at him. 'I'm supposed to be here to help, not cause more problems.'

Before Richard could stop her she tried to sit up, but the pain must have proved too much for she slumped back down again. He was checking the rapid heartbeat again when he realised that the three children were silently watching his performance, their fear and uncertainty mirrored in their eyes.

Explain things to children. Remember their active imaginations can exaggerate even normal confusion into fearful situations. Take the time to tell them what you are doing, especially when the unusual occurs.

He'd forgotten his own advice!

'Gran will be OK,' he assured them, his mind working overtime as he sought the words he needed. 'I think she's broken her arm, and because it's hurting her brain's telling her to go to sleep so she can't feel it. When the ambulance arrives the ambulance man will give her something for the pain—'

'Like a Panadol tablet? We've got some of those,' Margaret suggested.

'Like that, only an injection,' Richard told her. 'A tablet would be hard to swallow and the injection will work faster.'

All three nodded solemnly and Richard grinned, an

absurd feeling of relief flowing through him. Maybe
he hadn't lost his touch with kids after all!

'Now, what we have to do is make her comfortable.
How about you get a blanket?' he said to Jill, who
nodded and dashed off towards the back of the house.

'And—Mikey—you could grab two of those cushions
off the couch and bring them here. We'll put them under
your gran's feet.'

Margaret went with him and they each carried a
cushion back to him.

'Why?' Margaret asked, as he lifted the woman's legs
on to the cushions, then covered her with the blanket
Jill had produced.

'When you hurt yourself your body gets a shock and
begins to feel cold and shivery. Then your heart has to
beat faster so blood can rush around your body and warm
you up. We can help Gran's heart by keeping her warm.'
He tucked the blanket in, unwilling to cause the woman
more pain by moving her before the ambulance arrived.

'How do you know all these things?' Margaret asked,
obviously feeling he'd gone beyond the role of helpful
neighbour.

'I'm a doctor, that's how,' he reassured her. 'Lifting
her legs onto the cushions will help—'

'Because her blood can run downhill.' Mikey grinned
as he pointed this out and Richard smiled at him. All
three of the children seemed more relaxed, although the
older girl was unnaturally quiet and unhealthily pale.
Had she seen a loved one die? He tried to think how he
could distract her.

'The first thing you do in any accident is make sure
the injured person is breathing,' he told them. 'We can
tell Gran's breathing is OK because we can see her chest
rising and falling under the blanket.'

The twins bent lower over the recumbent woman but the older girl still hung back, worrying him with her remoteness.

'Then we check to see if the person's bleeding. Gran's lucky—there's no blood. So now I'll take her pulse to see how her heart's behaving. Jill, you're wearing a watch. Does it have a second hand?'

A faint pink flush crept into the pale skin and the girl nodded.

'Well, I want you to tell me when to start, then tell me thirty seconds later—that's when the second hand has gone halfway round the watch. Could you do that?'

She gave another nod, then she raised her wrist and studied her watch.

'Now!' she whispered in a hoarse voice, and the twins both turned to stare at her.

Richard started counting. His fingers had been monitoring Gran's pulse since he arrived on the scene, and he knew her heartbeats were a little fast but strong and regular. This exercise was for the child whom he sensed was 'different' in some way.

'Stop!'

The murmured word made him look up and he caught a shy smile on Jill's face. He was reminded of a young fawn he'd once seen, curious enough to want to come out of the shelter of the forest—wanting to trust the strange two-legged creature—yet held back by an instinctive wariness more powerful than curiosity.

'Gran's pulse is very good considering she's had a bad fall,' he told them. 'Thank you for timing me, Jill.'

She nodded at him and he knew she'd retreated again,

but she was definitely less tense—less shocked—than she'd been earlier.

'That's a car,' Mikey cried, and darted off towards the front door.

'It's not Marnie's car so it must be the ambulance,' Margaret told him with an earnestness that belied her years. He heard doors opening and voices, then looked up to see two attendants wheeling a stretcher through the front door.

He stood back and watched as they checked the woman's vital signs, jotted down their findings, slipped a pressure splint on her arm and then transferred her to the stretcher. The two men wheeled their patient towards the door and Richard and the children followed, Margaret reaching up to take his hand.

'We'll see if we can locate Dr Crail on the way to the hospital. If he's about we can take her to Clareville, otherwise it will be Weldon. Marnie on a case, is she? Where's young Kyle?' the older attendant asked.

Richard was about to explain that he knew nothing when Margaret answered in her 'grown-up' voice.

'Marnie went to Crosbys' to check on the new baby and Kyle has drum practice so Marnie was going to collect him when he finished. Gran was here so it didn't matter if she was late home.'

As she recited the information Richard tried to imagine the fiery-tempered woman he'd met yesterday explaining her plans so precisely.

'Well, I'll ring Marnie at Crosbys' or leave a message for her at the school and let her know where we've taken your gran,' the young ambulance bearer told the children as the stretcher slid into place and he closed the door. Then, as he made his way to the driver's side of the vehicle, he turned to Richard. 'You can stay with them until Marnie gets home?'

It was more a statement than a question and Richard found himself nodding.

The children stared at him. Sensing a wariness in them, he held up his free hand.

'I guess we'll manage until your mother gets home,' he said lightly, then he smiled and added, 'And I promise not to yell!'

The boy studied him for a moment, then turned towards the older girl.

'It'll be OK, Jill,' he said. He took her hand and led her down the passage. 'Let's get afternoon tea.'

Richard felt his own small charge tugging at his arm, urging him to follow. He let her lead him, for the first time taking in the comfortable area that must serve as the centre of the house. Lounge chairs were clustered near a wood-burning stove, and a dining table was set over by the glass walls so that the family could look down towards the creek as they ate. Bookshelves lined the walls and, in a far corner, huge cane baskets held an assortment of toys.

Don't banish your kids to a far part of the house for their fun and games—let them play near you, but insist they take responsibility for keeping 'their space' tidy.

Even his own sister had argued with him about that suggestion. She believed that children's play should be relegated to a part of the house as far as possible from their parents.

He was still admiring the ambience of the room with its polished timber floors and unpainted brick walls when the small girl tugged at his hand again. He looked down into the gentle brown eyes and smiled at her.

She studied him intently, then returned the smile.

'She's Marnie, not mother,' she told him, then dropped his hand and danced away to join her siblings in the kitchen.

CHAPTER THREE

AND Marnie came home an hour later—she and Kyle.

Richard was struggling up the hill with Margaret on his shoulders, Mikey dancing in front of him and the silent Jill tagging along behind—holding his shirt as carefully as a present. His wet shorts flapped around his legs, and water from Margaret's wet body trickled down his back and chest.

The twins had announced that they played until five-thirty when they had to come in for a bath and some quiet time before tea.

Children appreciate boundaries—they are happy with set routines and timetables.

He'd cast a surreptitious glance along the bookshelves while the children tidied the kitchen after their snack but hadn't seen any of his books, yet his words kept coming back to haunt him. Or did it simply prove that his books were common sense and that some people had plenty of their own? Perhaps the redhead and her husband didn't need him to tell them how to raise their kids.

'So, we'll show you the platypus,' Mikey had decided, when all three had changed into shorts and red T-shirts. 'It's in your part of the creek so that's why we don't swim there.'

'Or fall off the logs in case we frighten it,' Margaret added. 'Marnie forgot to tell you that yesterday.'

He could hardly let them go down to the creek on their own when he'd yelled at them the previous day for playing there. Besides, he was curious about the platypus. Why would the notoriously shy creature want to live anywhere near this many kids?

So, after watching Jill write a note on the whiteboard, he'd let them lead him down to the creek and along the bank, then had obeyed their orders to sit and be very quiet.

As they'd sat and waited he had felt the heat of the twins' bodies pressed one on either side of him, and some of the tension of the last few months was drawn out of him.

Then Jill had touched his shoulder and pointed, and he'd seen the quicksilver flash of wake across the water. When his eyes had focussed properly he'd glimpsed the brown fur and flat rubbery tail of the rare mammal and had felt the thrill of ownership. A platypus in *my* creek! Well, my rented creek!

Another flash and it had disappeared.

'We probably won't see it again this afternoon,' Mikey had told him. 'It can hold its breath for ever so long. Would you like to see the swimming hole?'

He had asked so politely that Richard had felt obliged to agree, and he'd scrambled along the bank to where the water was a deep, mysterious green.

'You know you must always be careful diving into creeks in case there are rocks or logs under the water,' he had said, wondering how the children's parents could let them swim here.

'Marnie used to dive down and check each time we swam, especially after rain,' Margaret had told him, 'but now Kyle does it instead.'

She had knelt down and put her hand into a hollow at the base of a thick river gum. Richard had thought of snakes and shuddered at the vulnerability of children—

so many dangers—then looked down as she unwrapped an old towel and revealed a mask and snorkel.

She'd looked up at him, her brown eyes full of hope, so he'd stripped off his shirt and shorts, stepped out of his sandals and, clad only in his briefs, checked the gravel-bedded creek. Once he was wet he had swum with them, marvelling at the agility of the lean, pale bodies as they had splashed and played and dived between his legs.

After the swim they'd sat on the bank, letting the still-fierce heat of the late summer sun dry their bodies. The children had identified the birds that flirted and sang above the creek and pointed out nests in the trees, and talked about all the wonderful things they were planning to do in the long Christmas holidays.

Marnie's first thought was that there'd been an accident and she ran down towards the little cavalcade. Then she saw laughter, not concern, in the four faces. She stopped her headlong rush and began to move more sedately.

Her new neighbour was bare-chested, water trickling down from Margaret's wet clothes and disappearing into the tangle of dark hair on his chest.

'Where's Gran?' she asked, to distract her thoughts from manly chests.

Shadows chased across their faces. The man lifted Margaret from his shoulders and set her down, before stepping forward to explain.

'She fell and broke her arm. The ambulance man was going to try to contact you so you could see her before you came home. She knocked herself out and Mikey ran across to get me.'

He must have seen her surprise for he smiled suddenly,

adding, 'Apparently an ogre of an adult is better than no adult at all.'

The smile wiped the darkness from his face, transforming him into a heart-stoppingly attractive man. It also set alarm bells ringing in Marnie's head. Discounting old friends who happened to be male and other women's husbands, men had disappeared from her life with the advent of the children so she had no in-built defences against smiling good looks or water-beaded bare chests.

'I'll phone the hospital,' she stammered, annoyed by where her thoughts had led.

'I think the first priority might be dry clothes for these three.'

Marnie looked down at the three uncertain faces and smiled reassuringly. They'd have been shocked by Gran's accident. Also, they seemed to have adopted the new neighbour but they wouldn't want to appear too friendly if she was still at war with him.

'Bathtime,' she reminded them, and shooed them up towards the house, pleased to hear their silence broken by Margaret's piping voice as she replied to Kyle's questions.

'Thank you for coming to their aid,' she said, keeping her smile in place. 'Would you like to come inside?'

He didn't reply immediately, but as she turned away he followed her.

She could feel his presence thudding against the nerve-receptors in her back—and knew it was diminishing the concern she should be feeling for her mother. She shouldn't have asked him in! She should have thanked him properly and let him go home.

She decided to have another go and turned back to face him.

'I'm sorry you were bothered,' she muttered at him, then quoted another of Gareth Gordon's 'rules', 'but I've always told them to call an adult if they need help.'

He half smiled and her heart, usually the most reliable of organs, skipped a beat.

'They were managing quite well without me,' he explained. 'Jill had already called the ambulance.'

Richard saw a look of total disbelief flash across her face.

'You mean Margaret—the little redhead.'

He shook his head, puzzled by her reaction.

'No, Jill,' he repeated, and held out his hand. 'About this high, dark hair, and grey eyes that are going to slay the men she meets when she's a little older.'

'Jill phoned?' she breathed, a shining kind of wonder lighting up her whole face. 'Jill called the ambulance and told them where to come?' she asked, more loudly this time. Then, seemingly oblivious of his damp clothes, she flung her arms around his neck and hugged him tightly.

'I knew it would happen one day! I knew if we just gave her time—!'

Excitement seemed to bubble out of her, overflowing in waves that beat against his skin and made his pulses stir.

Then she must have realised that she was dancing up and down in a stranger's arms and drew away stiffly. He watched the delicate flush of colour rise up beneath her skin and wanted to say, It's OK, I didn't mind being hugged.

In fact, he'd have liked to add, You can hug me any time, but that was ridiculous—besides, part of his mind was off on another tangent. Why was the child's phone call causing such jubilation?

Marnie felt the heat in her cheeks as she drew away from the man. She wondered what Dr Gordon would say about responsible mothers hugging men they'd barely met!

'I'd better phone the hospital,' she muttered, then fled down the passage, aware of his gaze following her. She could hear Margaret shrieking in the girls' bathroom and poked her head through the door to tell her to calm down.

She repeated the command to herself but it did little to still the unsteadiness of her heartbeat.

Gran was at Clareville, her arm set and resting comfortably. Dr Crail had left a message to say he wanted to keep her in hospital for a few days because he knew she wouldn't rest if she went back to the house. And Gran had left a message to say not to come rushing into town—she'd survive the night without visitors, thank you very much.

Marnie smiled as she hung up the receiver, then she remembered her own visitor and hurried back to the living area. Her neighbour was there, bent over and frowning slightly as he examined her books. Her own brow puckered for the man looked so at home in her big room—which was strange in a house where men were only transient presences and usually left no impression.

'My mother's "resting comfortably", as they say.'

He looked up and she noticed he'd pulled on his shirt. He must have started buttoning it absent-mindedly while he studied her bookshelves for the buttons were in the wrong holes, making one half of the front hang lower than the other.

'That's great,' he said. 'Will she stay "resting comfortably" for a few days? She'll need time to recover from the shock.'

'Dr Crail has already told her that. He's insisting she stay in.' She answered vaguely, part of her attention required to resist the temptation to cross the floor and fix his shirt.

He must have seen the focus of her eyes for he looked down and realised what he'd been doing. She watched his fingers undo the mismatched buttons, revealing a glimpse of dark hair curling on his chest. She remembered how his chest had looked bare, and felt an unfamiliar tingle in her blood.

'Come on!'

Margaret's voice brought her back to earth.

'Vegetables!' the little girl reminded her. 'You haven't got them out so Jill doesn't know what you want done.'

Marnie blinked and looked at Margaret. A strange disorientation had invaded her and she felt as if she'd been released from a spell.

'I'll be there in a minute,' she said, and moved towards their visitor.

'I know I've yelled at you and my children have shanghaied you into helping them but we still haven't officially met. I'm Marnie Ferguson.'

She held out her hand and felt his grip it strongly. His palm was cool and still slightly damp, but the touch of skin on skin sent her spinning back into the confusion she'd felt minutes earlier.

'Richard Cunningham!' he said crisply, and dropped her hand as if it might contaminate him.

'I've got to get dinner organised,' she told him, stepping back to put some space between them. 'Would you like a cup of tea or a cool drink, or have we taken up enough of your time?'

He seemed to hesitate, his grey gaze sliding across her

face then meeting her eyes with a question she couldn't understand.

'I'd better go!' The words were abrupt, matching his movement as he turned on his heel and headed for the door.

'Thank you coming to the rescue,' she called after him, then she turned to Margaret. 'See Mr Cunningham out,' she suggested, and watched the little girl skip after him and take his hand.

She should have been relieved, but she wasn't. In fact, if anything, she was jealous of Margaret's carefree acceptance of the man as a new friend. She found herself wishing she had a friend like him herself, but she could hardly go skipping after him and grabbing at his hand.

Why had Marnie Ferguson reacted with such delight when he'd said that Jill had phoned the ambulance? The question hammered in Richard's head later that evening while he boiled himself two eggs and spread them on toast, then ate this unsatisfactory snack. He must take himself to town and do some proper shopping!

He remembered the 'unused' quality of Jill's voice as she'd watched the time for him, then her retreat into silence throughout their adventures at the creek. Had she stopped speaking at some time? And, if so, why? Some kind of shock, perhaps? An accident in her past? He thought of Jackie's latest charity and the Christmas Day appeal. He'd seen plenty of children who'd suffered physical abuse, but Jill. . .? Part of his mind nibbled at the edges of the question. It was present, but not in the forefront of his mind.

In the forefront of his mind was an image of a red-headed woman reaching out her arms to encompass her children. He knew it was impossible but, for a moment there this afternoon, he imagined he'd actually seen love spilling out and touching those kids—seen it like a vapour, enshrouding and protecting them.

How ridiculous!

He made his way upstairs and settled at his desk. He couldn't see the kitchen or living area of the house from here, but he could see the front drive and he was only too aware that no second car had driven in. Nor had the children mentioned a father—but four virgin births might be pushing things! He grinned to himself, pleased that his depression of the last few weeks seemed to be lifting.

Now all he had to do was settle in to some serious work. Perhaps if he could become interested in a particular case? Could he begin with Jill?

Would it be appropriate to call over there later—when the children were in bed? He could enquire about the grandmother and try to work Jill into the conversation. Had their father left them—or been killed? Had she stopped talking then?

He frowned at his thoughts. He didn't want to start thinking of the neighbour's children as 'cases', and he wasn't entirely certain that his only interest was in the children.

Marnie read the twins a bedtime story, checked on Kyle—who was wrestling with a mountain of home-work—then inspected Jill's project. It was a coastal scene, a land- and sea-scape, modelled out of papier-mâché—two headlands with a bay in between. On each level of the model she'd drawn in the plants, animals and birds that inhabited the region, painting them down to the tiniest details.

'May I put it in the living room so the others can see

it in the morning?' she asked, and saw a quick smile as
Jill nodded.

The girl had artistic talent and Marnie longed to foster
it, but Jill wasn't ready to stay on in town for art lessons
just yet—in fact, she wasn't ready to do anything on
her own.

Marnie kissed her goodnight, then carried the model
out carefully and set it on the dining room table. Maybe
soon, she told herself, bending closer to discover tiny
ladybirds and ants drawn between fine blades of grass.

'Anyone home?'

The deep tones startled her, then she recognised
her neighbour's voice. Richard Cunningham, she
remembered.

'Come in,' she called, walking towards the front
entrance to welcome him. But was he welcome? Her
head was wary, but her heart played its own tune and
she hoped its reaction wasn't evident in her cheeks. She
was twenty-five—she should be past the blushing stage
by now!

'I called to ask how your mother was,' he said, and
she wondered if he'd jogged down the drive for his own
cheeks seemed to hold a hint of colour beneath his tan.

'I rang again and spoke to her. She feels a little bruised
and battered but otherwise OK.'

They were standing in the wide slate-tiled entry.
Marnie moved from one foot to the other, uncertain
whether to invite him further in or continue the conversation where they stood. It was safer where they stood!

'Do you want to come in—to sit down—or are you
just passing by?' she asked, cringing inwardly as she
heard the stupid words. Where would he be 'passing
by' to?

He hesitated and she imagined she'd overstepped

some invisible line drawn between them. Or was he wondering what Mrs Cunningham would say if he didn't go straight home? She was still considering Mrs Cunningham when he nodded with the same abruptness she'd noticed earlier.

She led him towards the sitting area and waved her hand towards a comfortable leather armchair.

'Feel along it before you sit,' she warned. 'The kids are pretty good about putting their toys away but it's amazing how often a Barbie doll or Spiderman finds its way down between the cushions.'

She watched him check then lower his long frame into the chair, and again she was struck by how at home he looked.

Get yourself out of here, Marnie! common sense urged.

'I was just about to make a cup of tea. Would you like one?'

She looked like a startled bush creature poised for flight, Richard thought. He never drank tea but heard his lips saying he'd enjoy a cup. The woman was bewitching him with her golden brown eyes, clear pale skin and dark red curls. He'd taken out plenty of more beautiful women, but none of them had seemed as vibrantly alive as this Marnie Ferguson—a married woman with four children!

He listened to the clatter of crockery in the kitchen and prayed her husband would come home. He'd be dark, Richard decided, with a quick reassuring smile like the one he'd seen Kyle flash at his sister that first day. A fellow who could become a friend, he told himself, then wondered why he didn't believe a word of it.

Marinie carried the tray back into the living room. She'd taken ten minutes in the kitchen—five to boil the kettle and make the tea, and the other five to stabilise her breathing and pulse rate.

She set the tray down on a table in front of his chair and waved her hand towards the pot, milk and sugar.

'Help yourself,' she suggested. 'The cake's a bit stodgy—it's practically all fruit. I'm working through an allergy programme with Mikey at the moment and have had to take sugar out of his diet this fortnight.'

'Hyperactive, is he?' The empathy in his voice surprised her. The man sounded as if he understood the difficulties of having a hyperactive child.

She watched him pour his tea and relax back into the chair with a large chunk of her stodgy cake in his hand. Her lips felt numb and her mouth dry but she had to talk. Silences between strangers were awkward and uncomfortable.

'The hyperactivity's not too bad, but he's asthmatic as well. When he has a bad bout of asthma the medication has him bouncing off the walls. I've decided if I can cut down on the frequency of the asthma attacks we'll all have a more peaceful life.'

'So, what foods have you eliminated so far?' he asked.

Marnie stared at him. He couldn't really be interested in Mikey's problems so why was he asking?

'I avoid artificial additives and food colourings for all the kids, and have had him off dairy products for years. Peanut butter's bad. I took him off all wheat products for a month but that didn't seem to make any difference, and the other kids were close to revolution because we all eat what he eats so we're back on normal bread and— But you wouldn't be interested—'

She remembered Margaret saying something.

'You're a doctor! I'd forgotten that. I couldn't think why a neighbour was being so polite.' She forgot about

Mikey as excitement she should have felt earlier rippled
through her.

'Are you opening up a new practice or going in with
Dr Crail? I can't understand why no one's mentioned it.
Most people in this area know things weeks before they
happen—or claim they do! The hills are awash with
psychics and soothsayers, although I suspect they're just
modern names for good collectors of gossip.'

He set down his teacup in its saucer and straightened
in the chair. Marnie knew immediately that Mikey's
asthma had been a better conversational subject. The
pleasant air of camaraderie had vanished and a wall of
ice was sliding up between them.

'I'm not here to practise and I'd prefer you didn't
spread it around that I'm a doctor. I've leased the house
as a retreat, an escape from the pressures of work in
Brisbane.'

He hesitated and Marnie shivered in the warm
December air—the invisible wall was sending out waves
of coldness.

'I'm only here for a couple of months over Christmas.
There's a project I must complete—a deadline to meet.'

'Oh!' she muttered. 'I'm sorry I jumped to the wrong
conclusion. We need a new doctor so desperately that I
thought you were the answer to all our prayers.'

And that could be taken other ways! she realised,
fighting the heat she felt flooding to her cheeks.

She glanced across the room and saw his dark brows
gather in a frown. If only she could make things comfortable between them once again. Buoyed by this thought,
she rushed to explain.

'The area is growing—not the town itself, perhaps,
but more and more people are buying properties in the
hills. In the sixties it was the domain of hippies and

flower-power people, and now the children of those days—having headed for the city as soon as they were old enough to leave home—are coming back. They're successful and wealthy so are able to commute from here to Brisbane or Sydney a few days a week to work, while their children have all the advantages of growing up in a beautiful area with clean air and unpolluted water. I suppose that's why you came.'

'Not for my children's sake,' he said, jolting her intestines with the quiet denial.

She didn't want to know about his children! Didn't want him to have any, if the truth were known! Perhaps she could ignore the remark.

'So, anyway, although Dr Crail manages to do the best he can he must be close to seventy and he doesn't want to keep working. The poor old fellow has to because no one seems to want to come to little towns like Clareville.'

'Which is why you found the idea of a new doctor in town so exciting?' he said, and Marnie imagined the ice was beginning to melt. 'I'm sorry to disappoint you but, as I said, I'll only be here two months.'

She opened her mouth to ask if he could help out for that length of time, then shut it again. He didn't want to be a doctor and she didn't want to fight with her neighbour.

But, damn it, they needed a doctor, especially over the Christmas holiday period when many of the weekend families would be here for six weeks over the summer school holidays. It would help Dr Crail, and might relieve some of the pressure on herself. When things were busy she was on call for Casualty and A and E at the hospital, as well as handling her normal midwifery practice.

'Would you cover for Dr Crail while you're here? Perhaps an occasional weekend?'

She saw his eyes darken before she'd finished asking and knew she'd made another big mistake.

'Someone must do that now!' he pointed out, his voice as cold and deep as the swimming hole in the creek.

'People drive to Weldon,' she said flatly. 'It's an hour each way over a dangerous, winding road.'

He made an exasperated noise and held out his hands in supplication.

'Look,' he declared, 'I've come here because other demands on my time were blocking this project. I'm not a GP, anyway. I'm a specialist. I'd help out if I could, but I've got to finish this work and get back to my real life.'

The words were brisk, bordering on belligerent, and Marnie wondered who he was trying to convince—her, or himself?

'It was just a thought,' she said, trying to shrug off the silly disappointment the conversation had produced. She felt he'd let her down in some way—yet he owed nothing to her or the Clareville community. In fact, if anything, she was still in his debt.

'I didn't thank you properly for taking care of the children,' she added, formally polite. 'I do hope they won't disrupt your work.'

He knew he'd killed the rapport which had grown between them earlier, and regretted it. She was so lovely, curled up in the big armchair—looking not much more than a kid herself. A kid with curves in all the right places. . .and lovely eyes. . .and hair so richly shining he wanted to run his—

He waved his hand dismissively, banishing the treacherous thoughts.

'I enjoyed spending time with them,' he said, and was surprised to find the statement was the truth. He remembered seeing her come home in the early hours of the morning, then tried to forget as a clear image of her legs as she'd peeled off her skirt flashed to the forefront of his mind.

'What do you do that you work such odd hours? Do you have a job at the butter factory?' he asked, hoping that common-sense questions would pull his thoughts into line.

And they might have if she hadn't flashed him a smile that pushed them straight back out again.

'No, I'm more in line with your business,' she explained, the smile still curling around the words. 'I'm a midwife so you can imagine the unpredictability of my life. My mother's been living with us on and off, but I'm encouraging her to get back to her own life. Being stuck on a ten-acre lot minding four kids after school is not a life for an active fifty-something. She has a house on the Gold Coast, and has been away following up on something. . . Today was her first day back.'

She was concerned about her mother, he guessed, seeing the golden-brown eyes grow dark with regret.

'And your husband? The children's father?'

She shifted in the chair, uncurling her legs and dropping her feet back onto the floor so she looked like a schoolgirl acting grown-up.

'I'm not married,' she said quietly. 'The twins' father never wanted them. And heaven knows who fathered Kyle and Jill—certainly not responsible members of the male species.'

Bitterness underscored the words, yet instinct told him that such an emotion was at odds with her nature. He felt concerned for her, yet affronted at the same time. Was she so promiscuous she didn't keep track of the men who shared her bed? Or was she one of those women to whom children were everything—a woman who had no need of a man in her life once procreation was achieved?

And that thought disturbed him even more!

CHAPTER FOUR

'TELL me about Jill?'

Richard's question echoed through the silence which had fallen between them as they sipped their tea. Marnie sighed and shook her head.

'Maybe one day she'll tell you herself,' she offered. 'All we know is that something happened in her life which must have been too terrible to talk about—'

'So she stopped talking?'

Richard's question was a husky murmur, as if he genuinely cared about the girl.

Marnie's throat grew tight and she nodded.

'But you must know when it happened—can't that help you work out what it was?'

The question disappointed her. For a fraction of time she had imagined she'd found someone who might understand how she and her mother felt about Jill.

'Why's it so important to know the details?' she demanded. 'Why is the medical profession obsessed by causes? Surely bringing up bad things must be horrific for a child—surely they must relive them as they tell about them, feel the agony and despair and the helplessness again. Why can't they just be left to heal in their own time—left to put the past behind them?'

She saw him blink as if her avalanche of defensive words had startled him.

'Psychologists and psychiatrists use a medical parallel,' he argued. 'They say an infected wound won't heal until all the infection has been drained from it, and that the mind works in a similar way.'

'But that parallel isn't necessarily true,' Marnie countered. 'Most small infections are cured from within. Antibodies fight the infection, forming pus with the dead cells, then the detritus is drained away by the blood. The body, left alone, will cure itself.'

'So, if one of your children is sick do you let time cure him or her, or do you head straight for your overworked and elderly Dr Crail and demand antibiotics?'

Marnie could feel his eyes boring into her, but she stood her ground.

'Antibiotics can only do so much,' she said staunchly. 'And as for the kids' ailments I usually insist on plenty of fluids and a few days' rest.'

She realised this wasn't entirely true and grinned at him, before continuing, 'Although, I must confess, if it's an infection like tonsillitis I go straight to the doctor, and I don't muck around with Mikey's asthma or Kyle's eczema. I have a medicine cupboard that would stock a small pharmacy.'

He smiled and shook his head.

'But you'll use time alone with Jill?'

It was a gentle question, but Marnie could feel the claws beneath the sheathed pads.

'Time and love and security,' she pointed out. 'She's come a long way already and it's been less than twelve months—'

'Twelve months is a big slice of time in a girl of that age,' he interrupted. 'Aren't you afraid that whatever it was is going down deeper and deeper into her psyche? Perhaps too deep to ever be dredged back up?'

Marnie straightened in her chair.

'I presume psychiatry's your speciality,' she said

coolly, so disappointed in the man she'd hope'd might be a friend that she wanted to throw something at him. 'And, no, I'm not worried about her psyche or any other weird bit of mumbo-jumbo. I'm worried about restoring normality to a little girl who's suffered some terrible trauma.'

She glared across the room, aware that he, too, had straightened and that his eyes had grown cold and hard.

'And my way is working!' she added. 'Jill proved that when she spoke today.'

Richard searched for words, but failed to find the ones he needed. With her eyes flashing anger and her cheeks blazing with her passion, she was beautiful in a way he felt rather than saw. Felt in his stomach, which had clenched into a knot, and in his loins, where a stirring reminded him that he was a sexual animal—currently without a mate.

'I'm not a psychiatrist!'

In his head the words had sounded sensible enough, but once they left his lips he realised how pathetic they were. She wasn't going to like him any more for what he wasn't—and she certainly didn't like him for what he was. For one mad moment he considered offering to help her friend, Dr Crail, then he remembered that he had a book to write and a deadline to meet.

He looked across at the wall of glass and saw the darkness of the night, unlit by city lights and garish neon advertising. Peace and solitude, that's what he'd sought. Time to get his life in order, to work out his priorities for the future and set reasonable goals—not impossible time schedules.

Then the very silence he'd been seeking snagged his attention. He glanced across at his neighbour, wondering why she hadn't asked what speciality he had studied—

wondering what she was thinking while his mind chased down its endless alleys.

Not thinking at all! he realised, and rose quietly to his feet. Her head had slipped sideways to rest on her arm, and her dark lashes were fanned across her creamy cheeks. She'd slid into sleep as effortlessly as a child, oblivious of the stranger within her walls and apparently unaware of the danger of such blind trust.

He was angry with her, angered by his own concern and scornful of the irresponsibility of such an action, yet he was mesmerised by her total relaxation and by the beauty of her face, wiped clear of all emotion by the soothing balm of sleep.

'She works too hard and often falls asleep in the chair.'

Richard spun around to find the older boy watching him from the entrance to the kitchen. How long had he been there? Did he keep a silent vigil over his mother whenever she had male visitors? And did she know and trust him to rescue her if the situation became sticky?

Maybe his anger and concern had been foolish, as foolish as the attraction he imagined he felt.

He watched the boy come quietly into the room, and saw him bend to gather up a soft tartan rug. With an ease which made Richard realise he'd done it often before he spread the rug over the sleeping woman, his hands softened by a love that seemed to radiate through the air.

'I must have bored her to sleep,' he said gruffly, and the lad flashed him a quick grin.

'Shouldn't think that's happened to you too often,' he said, with a man-to-man maturity that belied his age.

Richard found himself smiling.

'Very ego-deflating,' he agreed. 'Well, I'll be off. I guess I'll see you around.'

He held out his hand, and the teenager took it, shaking it firmly before releasing it.

'Thanks for this afternoon,' he said in a gruff, trying-to-be-grown-up voice. 'Marnie told me you'd come to the rescue.'

Richard felt an unfamiliar embarrassment wriggle across his shoulders.

'I didn't do much,' he muttered. 'The kids had already phoned for help.'

'Well, thanks, anyway,' Kyle repeated, then he led the way towards the front door. 'I've been mowing the bit of grass around your house. I'll keep doing it if you like.'

It was an olive branch.

'I'd appreciate that, but I'd like to pay you. Have you got set rates?'

The lad flashed him a smile.

'Marnie says we don't charge friends for favours, but she'd probably let me take five dollars for petrol.'

Friends?

Richard had followed him to the door but his legs felt heavy, as if his body was reluctant to leave this house which seemed to throb with life—even now when all but one of the occupants were sound asleep.

'It's a deal!' he said, and held out his hand again to seal it.

Kyle shook it and said goodnight, and Richard looked across at the hedge dividing the properties and considered the tunnel through the bushes.

Definitely not! he told himself. A man had to preserve some dignity.

He said goodbye to Kyle and set off up the drive, feeling the freshness of the night like cool water against his skin. Behind him in the thicker darkness the creek splashed and chuckled against its rock-strewn banks, and a kind of peace began to filter through his blood.

Not that peace would get his book written! he reminded himself two hours later. All it seemed to have done so far was atrophy his brain. He rubbed his eyes and felt the grittiness caused by lack of sleep. He'd go to bed and try again in the morning.

Marnie woke, cramped and uncomfortable, then realised she'd fallen asleep in the chair—again! She could vaguely remember talking to her new neighbour and, as she struggled to her room and threw herself down on the bed, she tried to remember him leaving.

She woke at six to the chorus of butcher birds, wondering why she'd slept in her clothes. No answer came to mind so she stripped them off, showered and dressed in the silver leggings and bright blue leotard she wore for her pregnancy exercise classes. Beyond her room she could hear the rustling noises of the children getting dressed for school, and she called good morning into each bedroom as she made her way to the kitchen.

'I hate getting up this early,' Margaret mumbled, shuffling into the kitchen with her hairbrush in her hand.

'It's worse in winter when it's cold and dark,' Marnie reminded her, running the brush through the tangled curls and easing them back into a tiny ponytail. Margaret had decided to grow her hair long like Jill's and no amount of persuasion could convince her that curly hair was better kept short.

'Of course, we could move into the village then you could walk to school and get up much later,' Marnie told her, snapping a band around the bunched hair.

'And leave the creek and the platypus?' Margaret cried. 'You know we couldn't do that!'

Marnie smiled. *Offer alternatives so the children are involved in decisions*. That was another of Dr Gordon's rules which appealed strongly to her, although she wasn't entirely certain the revered doctor would approve of the alternatives she sometimes offered!

'Well, if we stay here you have to get up early to make the school bus.'

'But it could pick up all the other kids then come out and get us,' Margaret pointed out. 'Jancy Cleeves doesn't get on till half past eight.'

Marnie smiled and hugged the little body.

'Perhaps you can talk to Bob about it,' she suggested, 'but I think doing the run the other way around would mean he'd have to get up much earlier and he'd have to come past our place twice because he lives further up our road.'

Margaret nodded, but the jutting bottom lip told Marnie she hadn't finished.

'I'll think of a way,' she promised. 'I hate being first on the bus and last off every single day, don't you, Jill?'

She darted out of Marnie's clasp and crossed the kitchen to grab Jill's hand. The older girl smiled at her, hesitating. Marnie remembered her neighbour saying that Jill had phoned the ambulance. She held her breath. Would she reply? Had yesterday been the beginning of the breakthrough they'd all awaited so eagerly?

Then Jill nodded and Marnie released the pent-up breath in a huge sigh. Maybe tomorrow, her optimism suggested. Margaret began setting the table for breakfast while Jill put the cereal, fruit, milk and bowls on the bench, ready for their help-yourself-style breakfast. Mikey appeared and began to make toast, and the day drifted into its normal pattern.

Until Kyle came in and grinned at her.

'Well, you sure impressed the new neighbour last night,' he told her.

Marnie frowned at him.

'What do you mean?'

Kyle's smile broadened.

'Falling asleep while he was talking to you,' he explained, waggling his finger at her. 'Not at all the thing a good-looking guy like that is used to, I would think!'

Marnie could feel embarrassment surging up from her toes, enveloping her in a chaotic discomfort.

'You're fooling!' she said, horror-struck. 'Tell me it's a joke!'

She pressed her hands against her flaming cheeks, but Kyle shook his head and chuckled gleefully.

'Dead to the world, you were, with him hovering over you looking as if he didn't know whether he should do a Prince Charming.'

'Do a Prince Charming?' she echoed weakly.

'You know,' Kyle teased. 'Bend over and kiss you awake.'

Marnie reached out, pretending to cuff his ears, but he danced away from her and joined the others at the breakfast table. She put the kettle on for coffee, trying to banish an image of Richard Cunningham's lips from her over-heated mind. But the image persisted, transferring effortlessly into the tantalising question of how it might have felt.

'Kettle's boiling,' Mikey said helpfully, and she switched it off, silencing the relentless shriek. He slipped the dirty cereal bowls into the sink while Jill carried the plate of toast to the table.

'Lunches!' he added in a quiet voice, as if willing to give her verbal clues to her usual routine but puzzled that she needed them.

Forgetting the coffee, she crossed to the refrigerator and began to pull packets of sandwiches out of the freezer. What would Dr Gordon—who'd advised her to organise her family so that the mornings could be pleasant, enriching experiences for all of them—say about her mooning in the kitchen while the kids missed the school bus?

She opened the pantry and added two pieces of fruit to each packet of sandwiches. She was about to pack the lunch-boxes, open and waiting on the window-sill, when Jill appeared and took over, calmly putting Kyle's larger lunch into his box and adding a bottle of juice—then packing her own box and finally the twins'.

Marnie watched her, present in the kitchen yet detached from all of them.

'Teeth,' Kyle reminded the twins, and they clattered out of the room, followed by Jill who'd closed the last lunch-box.

'He probably wouldn't have kissed you,' Kyle whispered as he walked past, his shoulders moving as he giggled at his own joke.

The words jolted Marnie back to earth. Of course he wouldn't have kissed her. He barely knew her. Normal men didn't go around kissing women they'd just met—especially women who had four children dependent on them.

She made a cup of coffee, nursing it between her hands as the kids came back and slid their lunch-boxes into their school bags. She carried her coffee to the front door, kissed them goodbye and watched as they made their way up the drive.

'See you this afternoon,' she called, and then, as they ran the last few yards—racing each other to the top—she glanced up towards the house next door.

She could see the window in one of the upstairs bed-rooms. The pane of glass was a golden blank in the morning sunshine, as blank as her recollections of the man next door's visit. She pictured him and tried to recall their conversation, searching through the scraps she did remember for a hint of wife and family.

The roar of an engine as the bus changed gear coming up the hill to her gate reminded her that this was a working day. She should call in and see her mother before the exercise class, then two postnatal visits and one home visit to help a newly pregnant young woman decide if she wanted a home or hospital birth. Whichever way she chose it was likely that Marnie would attend her.

The sister-in-charge at the hospital had midwifery training but she was too busy to follow the local women all the way through their pregnancy, and by the time they were due they'd grown so used to Marnie that they wanted her with them at the birth.

She sighed again. Another doctor in the town would mean an increase in staff at the hospital—maybe a mid-wife to deal with hospital births.

Another doctor in town! She frowned in the direction of her neighbour's house, then shook her head, annoyed by where her thoughts kept leading. She was already late and her usual leisurely routine was shot to pieces!

Richard heard the music blasting across the valley. He remembered his first day in the new house and wondered what the children were 'practising'. He hadn't seen any-thing of them for a few days and told himself he was pleased that they weren't intruding all the time. But while fences could keep out physical intrusion it was harder to build walls against the mental kind.

He ignored the noise for as long as he could, then

decided it was time to get out and breathe some of the fresh air he'd been seeking when he moved. He left the house, strolling as casually as he could down towards 'his' bit of creek. Once there he found the noise was fainter and realised that the children must be across the creek—perhaps in the old barn he could see beyond the trees.

He turned to walk back to the house, but the music beckoned him on—the music, and a child who didn't speak, and the knowledge that these children were a link to Marnie Ferguson.

For a week he'd steered clear of any involvement with his neighbours, telling himself it was the only way he'd get his work completed. But the word 'completed' was a joke. He'd barely started!

He stepped gingerly onto the logs that bridged the creek, remembering the thrill of fear such feats had generated in childhood. In all his books he encouraged parents to allow their children to experience this thrill— to push themselves to the edge but keep within the bounds of common sense and safety. Balancing, like swinging, helped the motor development of the brain, which in turn helped cognitive function. His neighbour had quoted that to him, although, as a trained nurse, she'd no doubt studied the developmental stages of children.

Children! They'd made him wealthy—brought him a fame he shunned by hiding behind another name. But did he really like them? He knew he had, back when he'd begun to specialise, but somewhere along the way they'd become objects of his study rather than small-sized people.

As he drew closer to the barn he could see, through gaps in the rough-hewn timber, the dancing figures of the neighbour's children, flashes of their red T-shirts making a moving collage against the old grey wood. And even now he couldn't say what had drawn him here—the children, or the fact they were his neighbour's!

He walked towards the open side of the old building, recognising it now as run-down cow bails. He didn't want the kids to think he was spying on them.

The music was building to a final crescendo of noise, and the little bodies spun with it. Kyle was able, performing his moves with a purposeful intensity. The twins were a little behind the beat, battling on with valiant persistence, but it was Jill who drew his attention. The child was dancing as if she were part of the music, her steps so light that she seemed to hover above the ground.

The final notes rapped out and the scene became a tableau as the performers stilled, then each child dropped to one knee with arms outstretched, saluting an invisible audience.

Richard clapped, unable to stop his reaction. Four faces turned to stare at him, then smile with varying degrees of acceptance.

'Did you see it all? Do you think we're good?'

It was Margaret who hurried towards him, asking the questions in an anxious voice.

'I saw enough to think you're very good,' he assured her, reluctantly accepting the sweat-dampened hand she held out to him. 'Are you having an end-of-year concert at school?'

Mikey shook his head, and Margaret was about to speak again when Kyle broke in.

'It's something private,' he said quickly.

'But how can we ask him if he'll drive us if he doesn't know what we're doing?' Margaret demanded, and Richard saw the older boy colour uncomfortably.

'Jim said he'll drive us,' he mumbled, and turned away, busying himself with the player.

'But only once,' Mikey pointed out.

Richard watched the interplay between them, interested in the democratic way each child seemed to be allowed his or her say. He could use that in his chapter on family decisions. Kyle might be the eldest but the others weren't cowed by his seniority. He filed the thought away.

'We might get enough going once,' Margaret said, her voice belying the hope in the words.

'Perhaps you'd better tell me more,' Richard said, directing his words towards the silent Jill.

The others turned towards her, their faces expectant.

'It's the Sunday markets,' she said, then closed her lips into a tight line.

No one spoke, but Richard was aware that Kyle had turned to stare at his sister. He was the only one who hadn't heard her speak the day of the accident.

'You'll perform there?' He asked the question then held his breath, caught up in the tension distilled like perfume in the old building.

Jill nodded and Margaret started towards her but Kyle held up his hand. Pretend it's normal, was his unspoken message.

'We're going to busk,' he explained. 'We want money to buy Marnie something special for Christmas. Gran was going to drive us but, although she's out of hospital, her arm's in plaster and she can't drive at all. We asked Jim and he said he'd take us this coming Sunday, but the following week is out for him—'

'There are only three Sundays before Christmas and we thought we'd get more money if we could go twice—' Mikey interrupted.

'So Kyle thought, if we asked really politely, you might take us,' Margaret finished.

'But only once, of course,' Kyle added, looking acutely embarrassed that his plan had come to light rather sooner than he'd expected. 'You see, if it was you, we could tell Marnie—'

'Tell Marnie what?'

Her voice made them all spin around and Richard wondered if he looked as guilty as he felt. More memories of childhood! That feeling of guilt when caught unexpectedly—even when he'd been doing nothing wrong!

He imagined he could feel the beseeching eyes of the children focussed on his shoulder-blades. Well, he didn't have to play along. . .

'Tell Marnie I've asked your brood to come with me to the markets on Sunday week. I've heard the craftwork is excellent. I want to buy some Christmas gifts and I'm sure they'll be able to point out the best stalls.'

He's asked the children but not me! Disappointment, as sharp and bitter as the taste of lemons, made her lips tighten.

'It means you'll be able to sleep all day if no one has a baby,' Margaret offered, her voice indicating what a treat this should be.

'How nice!' Marnie said lamely, uneasily aware that they seemed to be waiting for her to leave. 'Well, I just walked down to check on you.' She nodded at her neighbour. 'Thank you for offering to take them with you. They'll enjoy the outing.'

'And I'd have enjoyed it, too,' she muttered to herself as she walked away. 'But you wouldn't think of asking me, now would you?'

'Do you always talk to yourself?'

She jolted to a halt. That uncaring devil of a man had followed her out of the barn.

'Yes, I do!' she snapped at him. 'In fact, my most satisfying conversations are always with myself.'

'That's probably because you don't argue back,' he pointed out, falling into step beside her and making the wide stretch of paddock shrink to telephone-box proportions.

They reached the creek and he held out a hand to help her up onto the logs. She didn't want to take it, but it would look churlish to refuse. Their fingers touched, then linked and she forgot everything she'd ever known as a strange electricity burnt across the surface of her skin.

She glanced up and saw his eyes, silvered in intensity, graze across her face and focus on her lips. Held by some bond she didn't understand, she touched her tongue to the upper one and moistened the dryness her short panting breaths was causing.

'Don't argue back!' he repeated in a rusty kind of voice, then his head bent forward and he brushed his lips across hers—touching, caressing, teasing—then seized on her mouth with a powerful hunger she recognised only because it matched her own.

'Why are you standing there staring at the water?'

Margaret's voice brought her out of her trance. She pressed her fingers to her lips, remembering the torrid heat of that kiss and a kind of muttered commentary her new neighbour had made until he'd raised his head and roundly cursed them both for their folly—before striding off across the logs and up the hill to his new home.

And he was right! It had been folly. Folly to react to him—to behave like some sex-starved creature willing to kiss any chance stranger who strayed across her path.

'Are you thinking?' Margaret persisted, but before Marnie was forced to reply the others joined them, chattering excitedly about their projected outing.

Not that they enjoyed the markets much when she took them! In fact, they usually started chanting 'Boring!' to her after the first hour. The thought brought her back to earth with a thud. Maybe they were excited because they were going with Richard—she thought his name with only a slight rise in her inner temperature—maybe they needed more regular male company.

But not Richard Cunningham's! her heart warned.

'Well, don't get too attached to him,' she mumbled, more to herself than to the children who were following her across the logs. 'He's only here to complete his project—whatever that might mean—and then he'll be heading back to the bright lights of the city.'

CHAPTER FIVE

RICHARD went to bed well pleased with the amount of work he'd done, though less satisfied with the content. Considering that he'd had to force himself to concentrate—to focus his mind on writing in an attempt to banish the image of Marnie Ferguson's lips—ten pages wasn't bad, even if it was a little bland. He'd do some revisions in the morning and fax the completed text through to Jackie—see what she made of it.

With this decided, he settled his head on his pillow and closed his eyes.

And memories flooded his mind. He could feel the texture of her skin against his, could see the tip of her pink tongue dart out to moisten her top lip, could taste that faint saltiness of that unbelievable kiss.

What on earth had possessed him to kiss a woman he barely knew? He rolled over onto his other side, telling himself to think about chapter four—about the perfect relationship between parents and children he hoped to convey in his book.

She seemed to have a good relationship with her children—from what he'd seen of it—and, apart from Jill, the youngsters all seemed well adjusted. Perhaps he could think about Jill—about the silence that was so unnatural for a child.

He heard a engine start up then grumble to life, and recognised the sound of the old Volvo. He grimaced as he thought of his neighbour heading off to another

71

delivery. It had been after two when he'd gone to bed. Who'd be a midwife?

Noises in the night carried clearly so he knew when the car reached the top of her drive. The harsh grating sound that followed made him sit up. Had she taken her foot off the clutch too soon, or had something worse happened? He listened to the silence. Whichever way she turned he should have heard the car as she drove away.

Pleased to have something to divert his mind from kisses, he leapt out of bed, pulled on his shorts, grabbed the torch he kept by his bed and headed out of the house.

He could hear her cursing as he made his way up the drive.

'Trouble?' he called.

'I think it's finally died on me!' she growled at him, her voice still thick with sleep.

She had the bonnet up by the time he reached her and he shone the torch into the engine.

'I know absolutely nothing about car engines,' he admitted, when his torch had failed to find any obvious loose lead that might have made a hero of him. 'How far do you have to go? Would you like to take my car?'

She looked at him in horror. In the moonlight her skin shone with a clear translucence which made him want to touch it. And her eyes were as dark and velvety as the night sky.

'Drive that huge, glistening new machine? You've got to be joking! I've usually got Mum's car as a back-up, but I left it in town for a service while she's out of action with her arm. I suppose I'll have to go back down to the house and phone Albert. He runs the local taxi service and will probably charge me some exorbitant rate for getting him out of bed.'

Her voice brought him back down to earth. Or almost

back to earth for he heard himself saying, 'That's ridiculous. I'll take you wherever you have to go. If it looks like a quick birth I can wait and bring you home, otherwise you can call on Albert in the morning.'

She glanced at him then looked away, shutting the bonnet of the car with hands that seemed to shake a little.

'Rescuing my kids from predicaments is one thing, but offering lifts to an isolated farm in the early hours of the morning is going beyond the call of neighbourly duty. But I might use your phone to call Albert, if that's OK. Your house is closer than mine.'

She headed off down his drive as if demons were chasing her, and he remembered that she had a labouring patient waiting for her.

'I'll drive you,' he repeated firmly when he caught up. 'The time you save might make the difference between your being at the birth or the poor husband having to deliver the child.' He took her elbow and steered her towards the garage before she could object again.

'You're right about saving time,' she admitted as she buckled her seat belt. 'And Anne doesn't even have her husband with her. He's off overseas somewhere at present. The babies weren't due for six weeks. Could we stop by the car for my bags?'

'Babies? How many babies are expected?' He closed the door and started the engine. 'And why the hell are you going along with a home birth in a multiple pregnancy? Maybe if she lived in town where specialist attention is only a few minutes away—'

'There's no specialist attention in this town. There's medical help—sometimes—and there's me. And, for your information, she didn't plan a home birth. In fact, she intended moving across to the Gold Coast to be near her specialist tomorrow.'

She was fired up again, as if his presence sparked anger as naturally as a flint sparked flame. Combustible, this redhead—but she had the sweetest lips. . .

He dragged his mind back to the present and pulled up beside the Volvo.

'I'll get out. Is it just the bag?'

For a moment she didn't answer and he touched her lightly on the arm.

'Yes— Well, there are two bags. They're on the back seat.'

Marnie watched him uncoil himself from the car and move with long, athletic strides towards her battered old wreck. The last thing she'd wanted was to spend more time with this man, but she'd been managing all right until he touched her.

She rubbed at her arm. Why was it happening? Why now? Why this man, not some other? She didn't particularly like him—the little she knew of him. He was bossy and self-opinionated and he'd yelled at her kids.

'Do you carry all that gear around whenever you go out on call?' he asked after he'd stowed her bags safely in the back and they were heading towards the Williamsons' property.

'If it's a planned home birth the women always have lists of what they'll need on hand, but even in those cases I find it easier to take everything in case they're not prepared.'

'Which highlights the advantages of hospitals!' her chauffeur remarked in a deliberately neutral voice. 'And even though there's no specialist there's a hospital in town. Why didn't your patient call the ambulance?'

She sighed. City folk rarely understood the different dynamics out here in 'the bush'.

'She did. It's at a road accident on the range between here and Weldon. Dr Crail's up there as well. A car's gone over the edge with people trapped inside.'

He muttered something unintelligible and shook his head.

'So you're left to handle a pre-term delivery of twins in an isolated farmhouse.' He sounded angry. Did he think she couldn't cope?

'Midwives have been delivering babies since time began,' Marnie told him. 'Men didn't get into the act until they discovered there was money to be made out of it!'

'Ouch!' he said, and she turned in time to see a smile curling the visible corner of his lips. It made his profile look particularly appealing. She turned away quickly, refusing to be diverted by an appealing profile.

'Anyway, the ambulance will eventually arrive. All I have to do is hold the fort until it comes—'

'Great! Then you can have the option of delivering the twins in the back of a moving vehicle. That's real photo-in-the-paper, heroine-of-the-day stuff, isn't it!'

She swung back towards him.

'I'd be doing my job, nothing more and nothing less,' she retorted. 'And out here—' Damnation! His attention was on the road—but he was smiling! 'You said that to see if I'd bite?'

The smile broadened.

'You do seem to fire up quite easily,' he replied. 'Whether in support of your local medico or in defence of your children. I figured a light prod at your career would probably bring some response.'

The cheek of the man! He barely knew her and here he was making snap judgements. She folded her lips into a tight line to prevent them thrusting her deeper into the mire, and looked out into the inky blackness beyond the yellow glow of the headlights.

They could be anywhere, she decided. Two travellers making their way through the starlit night. A glance at her driver showed him frowning now as he followed the curves in the unfamiliar road. She'd noticed a little line between his eyebrows just before he'd kissed her and had wondered, fleetingly, if he frowned a lot.

'Which way?'

The question made her blink. She'd been imagining her fingers smoothing at the crease—wiping away his concerns.

'Right—no, left!'

He turned towards her.

'Sure of left or would you like another guess?' he asked in such mocking tones that she decided she'd rather thump him between the eyebrows than smooth away his cares.

'Definitely left!' She muttered the words at him as an awareness of his body, of his closeness, flooded through her. 'It's three kilometres from this turn to the causeway, then the property is the third gate on the right after the causeway.'

She saw his lips move and guessed he'd been about to tease her once again, then had thought the better of it.

'Do you ever catch up on your sleep after call-outs like this?' he asked. 'With four kids it must be difficult.'

The sympathy in his voice weakened her, but instinct told her to resist her strange attraction to this man while common sense began to wonder if it was a hormonal thing—an unprogrammed glitch in her well-ordered life.

'When my mother's at home it's not so bad,' she said calmly. 'And as the children get older it gets easier. Kyle's very responsible.'

'Does he mind being the "responsible" one?'

He asked the question she was always asking herself, and she turned towards him, forgetting she was trying to keep her distance from her new neighbour.

'I don't know,' she admitted quickly. 'It worries me no end because I don't know how boys think. Did you come from a large family? Were you the eldest? It's the next turn on the right. Do you think he might resent it? He says not, if I mention it, but he'd say that to be polite.'

'From what I've heard, teenagers rarely do anything they don't want to do—certainly not to be polite,' he assured her.

He slowed the car, then swung right between two painted posts. The car rattled across a cattle grid and onto a gravel surface. He was driving slowly now, watching the road and alert for whatever animals the grid kept in, but his mind puzzled over the woman who sat beside him.

She had distanced herself from him earlier—his fault for teasing, he supposed—but once he mentioned one of her children she was transformed immediately into an eager, questioning, worrying mother. Maybe he should be dealing with male and female parents separately in his book—or dealing with the different roles the two parents undertook. Would a father who was doing all the nurturing while his wife worked have reacted the same way?

'You can stop by the front steps.'

He braked abruptly and reached out to steady his passenger as she jolted forward.

'Sorry!' he said, relishing the warm softness of her skin beneath his fingers. 'Your questions led my thoughts off at a tangent. Are you OK?'

He brought the car to a standstill at the foot of the steps and looked towards her, then withdrew his hand reluctantly from her arm. She nodded hesitantly in response and he almost kissed her again, but the moment was lost. She turned away from him, unsnapping her seatbelt and pushing it off her shoulder.

'Anne must be inside somewhere,' she said, opening the car door and thrusting out her slim legs. 'I'll need my bags.'

'You go on in—I'll bring them,' he offered, and watched her hurry around the front of the car, take the steps up to the verandah two at a time and disappear into the house.

What was it about this woman that distracted him so much?

Marnie found Anne hunched in a knee-chest position on the double bed, muttering quietly into her pillow.

'Talking to someone?' she asked quietly, not wanting to startle her patient with her presence.

'I'm alternating "I will not panic" with "I'll kill Jim when he gets back",' Anne told her. 'Thank God you're here. The contractions have been getting stronger and stronger, closer and closer, and all I could think of was the cord getting tangled if I had to deliver them myself. I remembered enough from my brief stint in the labour ward to know this position would help if the cord pro-lapsed—'

She broke off abruptly, gasping as pain pulled the air from her lungs—rolling over to her side then onto her back as she sought relief from the strength of the contrac-tion. Marnie heard Richard come in and turned to retrieve the smaller bag. Mentally she listed off the procedures. Check foetal heart rates first, then Anne's blood pressure and pulse—

'I'll help—just tell me what to do.'

She spun towards Richard, startled by the offer, then remembered that he was more than a spare pair of hands—he was a trained pair of hands.

'There's a small oxygen tank in there, with tubes and mask. Could you set it up by the head of the bed somewhere in case it's needed? I put the gear out of the smaller bag on a table—the dressing-table will do if you clear it. Would you mind?' She didn't wait for him to answer, too intent on her own job. 'Then spread that rubber sheet on this end of the bed, with towels over that and a clean sheet over the lot.'

She held Anne's wrist during the next contraction, noting the beads of sweat across her patient's upper lip. When the contraction ended, Marnie bent to find the foetal heartbeats.

'Still two babies in there!' She smiled her reassurance at the woman. 'You've done brilliantly so far, Anne. Now we'll do what we can to help. I've even brought along a support person for you. Richard, Anne might like a sip of water. Could you find the kitchen and bring some back? I'd also like a dish of water, a bucket for rubbish and you might wet one of those flannels from the bag. Support people mop brows, you know.'

He looked slightly bemused as he left the room and Anne chuckled.

'And who's Richard? Were you out on a date?' she asked as Marnie examined her.

'A date? What's that?'

'Something that leads to this kind of torture,' Anne

groaned, Richard forgotten in the new wave of pain. 'I need to push, Marnie, I know I do.'

'Pant instead if you can!' Marnie advised. 'You can push soon. You're ten centimetres dilated and I can feel number one in position, head down like a good little girl or boy, but the head hasn't crowned.'

Richard returned at that moment and Marnie introduced him. He helped Anne into a semi-reclining position and tucked the wedge and pillows behind her back, then held the water to her lips.

She gulped at it, then pushed the cup away as her distended belly rose in another contraction. Marnie was aware of Richard moving to support Anne, holding her hand and talking quietly to her.

'The head's appeared. No prolapsed cord, Anne.' She checked the foetal heart rates, then examined Anne again, noticing that the baby's head was becoming more visible with each contraction. She crossed to the basin of water and scrubbed her hands with the brush and soap she carried in her bag.

Richard was talking quietly to Anne, saying, as Marnie returned to her patient, 'When I was training we had a tutor sister who prided herself on delivering babies with beautiful heads. "It's all in the delivery, Doctors," she would say. "Let the wee thing take his time." I didn't realise until years later that a controlled birth also lessened the risk of lacerations for the mother.'

Marnie glanced up, looking from Richard to Anne.

'You've blown your cover,' she said softly.

He grinned at her.

'I doubt it,' he said, and nodded towards Anne, whose entire being was focussed on the birth process.

It reminded Marnie of where her thoughts should be centred. She was too busy to be beguiled by a saucy grin.

'The head's crowned,' she told her patient. 'You're doing well, Anne. Try to listen to your body—let it tell you what to do.'

Her hands moved without conscious orders from her brain, reaching out as the baby's head flexed and then taking the weight and lifting slightly as it extended. She felt for the cord, found it encircling the neck—slack not tight—and looped it carefully over the head. She reached for the moist sponges she'd set out on a cloth close by and wiped the tiny face.

Anne groaned with effort and the first shoulder slid out. Marnie moved the slippery body slightly to prevent the posterior shoulder tearing the perineum.

'Take it slowly,' Marnie murmured. 'We're nearly there—you're a champ, Anne. It's a little boy.'

The baby gave a lusty cry as Marnie lifted him but any maternal delight was cut short as Anne's uterus contracted again and she had to concentrate on her pain. Marnie looked at Richard.

'Can you remember how to cut the cord, Dr Cunningham?'

She saw him react with a tiny jolt of shock, but his face told her he'd been as moved by the miracle of birth as she always was.

'Clamp each side and cut in the middle,' he mumbled to himself, moving swiftly to the end of the bed and finding what he needed among the equipment he'd laid out.

He pulled on gloves and performed the task neatly, but she was certain his fingers had been shaking. One part of her mind was asking why he didn't practise— or wasn't practising at the moment—while the other part was concentrating on her first assessment of the baby. Skin colour, muscle tone, heart rate and breathing all seemed OK. She'd have more time to check him later.

'All done,' Richard said quietly, stripping off his gloves. 'What next?'

'I think you're left holding the baby,' Marnie told him, as she swaddled the infant in a warm cloth. 'Hold him near your body for warmth and close to Anne so she can see and touch him if she wants to. I have to check on what's happening to number two.'

She bent over Anne, auscultating the foetal heartbeat then feeling the swollen abdomen to see if she could determine the second child's position. Anne's contractions were still strong, but Marnie sensed she was tiring. The second twin was in a breech position. Sometimes a baby would somersault of its own accord and come head first down the birth canal in the accepted manner.

And sometimes it would insist on coming legs or bottom first, Marnie reminded herself as the vagina opened wider to reveal the little bottom pushing its way out into the world.

She scrubbed her hands again and drew on gloves. Anne was quiet now, moaning slightly as she pushed, her entire being concentrated on expelling this second child from her womb.

'Sounds like the ambulance arriving,' Richard said quietly, but Marnie was absorbed in freeing the legs, drawing down first one and then the other.

'It's a little girl,' she told them, not looking up as she tried to get a finger into the baby's mouth to prevent the head locking during delivery. Anne was crying out with each push while Richard soothed and encouraged her. And gently, gently, Marnie helped the head emerge.

'Super midwife does it again!' a deep voice said.

'Bit late for the cavalry to be arriving,' she replied, without turning to see the ambulance attendants. She wiped the scrunched pink face and cleared the airway.

'You want to hold her while I cut the cord?' she asked Anne, and saw the look of dazed wonder on the new mother's face.

Anne's hands trembled as she clasped her daughter against her stomach. Richard held the little boy close and Anne looked from one to the other, as if unable to believe she'd produced these marvellous creatures.

Marnie clamped and cut the second cord and then, as Anne lifted the child to her breast, she spread a clean warm sheet over mother and baby. It was a hot summer night and the newborn infant would draw warmth from her mother's body, but the slightest breeze could chill her.

'Are you fellows in a hurry?' Marnie turned to the attendants who shook their heads.

'We've had more than our share of emergencies tonight,' the older one assured her. 'As long as the babies are OK, Mrs Williamson will travel easier if she's all fixed up before she leaves.'

'My thoughts exactly,' Marnie agreed. 'The babies are fine. I'll do an initial assessment and even write up some of your paperwork for you, if you'd like to make some tea. I think we could all do with a cuppa.'

'They seemed eager to get out of here,' Richard remarked as the two newcomers headed out of the bedroom.

'Don't most men still consider childbirth "women's business"?' Marnie asked. 'Those men have probably delivered nearly as many babies as I have but they still shy away from it.'

'Maybe it's a mystique thing,' Anne suggested dreamily, her fingers touching first one then the other little head.

'Bull!' Marnie muttered as she massaged Anne's abdomen to help the expulsion of the placenta. 'They just refuse to accept that it's a messy and painful outcome of something they thought of as a bit of fun or pleasure.'

'For a midwife, you're a terrible cynic,' Richard objected. 'And you're wrong. Most men these days insist on being present at the birth of their children.'

'Oh, they like the end result well enough, love boasting about their son or daughter, and they're eager enough to be present at the birth of their own children—but to be present at someone else's birth? That's different.'

Richard watched her work, attending to Anne and cleaning up with neat, unfussy movements. He watched the movement of Anne's belly contracting beneath the sheet. Third stage of labour, expulsion of the placenta, he remembered. Could take up to an hour. In his arms the baby stirred and he looked down to see dark blue eyes gazing impassively up into his face.

He was still studying the perfection of the tiny face when Marnie's voice made him raise his head. She was saying his name and by the look of things he'd missed the the third stage of labour altogether, such had been his fascination with the baby he cradled in his arms.

'I'm taking young madam so let Anne cuddle her son for a moment.'

He frowned, puzzled at first by what she meant. His arms tightened instinctively around the child and he felt a fierce, protective urge tugging at his intestines.

'I need to check on the little girl and wrap her for her journey to town,' Marnie told him, her dark eyes soft with understanding. 'And Anne hasn't said a proper hello to her son. She was busy when he arrived.'

Feeling a complete fool, he waited until Marnie had taken the little girl, then he passed 'his' baby to its mother. He straightened up, intending to get up off the bed, but Marnie shook her head.

'Stay there,' she murmured so only he could hear. 'Anne's very tired.'

He moved closer to the woman and put his arm around her shoulders.

'Thank you!' Anne whispered through tears which now flowed freely down her cheeks. 'For being here with Marnie. For holding me and helping me. I'd have liked Jim to have been here to see his babies born, but having you was better in some ways. I had a man to lean on, but I didn't have to worry about how he was taking it all.'

She snuggled against him.

'We'd thought of Robert for a boy's name, but I think we'd better call the young man Richard now.'

He felt the glow begin deep inside his stomach—as pleased as he'd been in his student days when someone had made the same promise. Marnie came back to the other side of the bed, the baby girl wrapped snugly.

'Can you hold two at a time?' she asked Anne, and bent over to settle the second baby in the cradle of Anne's free arm. 'They're early and small, but you must expect that with twins,' she told the new mother, who was gazing in awe at the babies. 'But they both breathed normally and their colour is good. They'll be fine.'

Richard watched Marnie reassuring her patient, seeing the shadows cast by the bedside lamp darken her eyes to mysterious pools. He began to understand why midwives had such a long tradition. At various times he'd felt panicky and shaken by what was happening yet this woman had radiated confidence, had calmed and soothed and encouraged. . .

'Tea's up!'

The loud call broke the spell.

'Do you want tea?' Marnie asked Anne.

'Not if it means putting my babies down,' Anne told her. 'I'll wait till later, thanks.'

Richard watched as she positioned the tiny mouths close to her nipples. To his amazement the boy's mouth opened, seeking sustenance or comfort. The baby girl nuzzled her lips against the dark aureole but showed less interest in food than her brother.

'I can't believe it,' he muttered, when she, too, latched onto her mother's breast.

'In a busy hospital situation the babies are often whisked away to be weighed and bathed and dressed,' Marnie said quietly, correctly diagnosing his surprise. 'You don't always get the opportunity to see their instincts working for them. Do you want a cup of tea?'

He nodded, his eyes still on the two neonates, his mind fired with a new and wondrous idea.

'Milk and sugar?' Marnie asked.

He nodded again, unaware of the question. He'd forget the parents and partners! It was too far removed from his usual field, anyway! He'd write about the newborn. . .about birth and birthing. . .about bonding. . .

He took the cup of tea she passed him and sipped at it.

'Ugh! That's revolting!' he spluttered, straightening up so that he didn't spill the hot brew on Anne. 'It's got sugar in it.'

As he glared accusingly at Marnie she smiled. Had she guessed he hadn't heard her question?

Then suddenly he found himself smiling back—found himself smiling at her as if they were alone on the top of a mountain, not in a warm crowded bedroom with tiny babies and ambulance men and a tired but glowing new mother.

'Time to get this show on the road,' she said quietly, setting down her teacup and moving towards Anne. 'Richard, you take one baby to the crib and I'll take the other. You guys help Anne onto your stretcher.'

He was disappointed by a brusqueness in her voice. He'd felt that moment of communion so strongly that he'd been certain she'd shared it—but now he was just another pair of hands as she organised the safe despatch of her charges.

'I'll come and see you in the morning,' she promised Anne when both babies were tucked into the crib.

Anne looked towards the window. 'I think it's morning now,' she said, her smile adding a luminous radiance to her tired face.

She held out both her hands, one to Marnie and the other to Richard.

'Thank you both,' she murmured, 'so very, very much!'

Her voice caught and tears glistened in her eyes. Richard felt his own eyes moisten unexpectedly and he grinned to hide his emotion. He followed the little procession of crib and stretcher out into the dawn and watched the attendants load Anne and the babies.

As the vehicle pulled away he turned towards Marnie, bearming with the satisfaction that comes from a job well done. She saw his smile, read his pleasure and then abruptly turned away from him, hurrying back into the house. But not before he'd seen the shadows of a dreadful sadness in her eyes.

CHAPTER SIX

MARNIE cleaned up swiftly and efficiently, sending Richard to wash the teacups and tidy the kitchen while she restored the bedroom to a pristine condition. And all the time her heart felt as if it were cracking wide open. The job done, he loaded her gear into the back of his big vehicle then he opened the door for her and took her arm to help her up into the seat.

Was it contact with another human being that broke the dam of her control, or was it this particular man?

She asked herself that as the tears began to slide down her cheeks, one clear thought in the muddle of her mind. Then he put his arms around her and folded her close against his chest, murmuring soothing nothings that made her cry harder until the pent-up grief she hadn't known she'd held was all cried out and she could pull herself away from him and scramble, damp and embarrassed, into the car.

He shut her door and came around to get in beside her, starting up the engine and driving off without a word.

His silence made her feel increasingly stupid—as if by not demanding an explanation he was forcing her to speak.

'I deliver babies all the time and never cry,' she told him, staring out at the grey shapes of the mountains in the lightening landscape. 'It must have been because they were twins.'

His silence continued but the atmosphere had changed.

'My sister was five months pregnant when they

discovered she had breast cancer.' The words were
drawn out of her, whispered into the crisp morning air.
'The doctors wanted to abort the pregnancy and start
treatment immediately. She refused, knowing that any
treatment would only prolong not save her life. Then
they wanted to induce the twins at six months, for the
same reason, but she said no again. That's when her
husband left her.'

A quick audible intake of breath made her turn
towards Richard, but his eyes were on the road ahead
and his face showed no emotion. It made it easier for
her to keep talking.

'He couldn't accept that she hadn't long to live anyway—couldn't understand her decision to give the
unborn babies a better start in life rather than give him
more time with her.'

She saw him nod, but didn't know which side he
might have taken.

'She had a difficult birth. The disease had weakened
her and the room was full of specialists. Mum and I
were too frightened for her to argue with the experts,
but I know now we could have made things easier for
her if we'd done it differently.'

'A home birth?' he asked, interested, not cynical.

'Perhaps not,' Marnie replied, 'but in a birthing suite,
not a labour room, with a hot bath and not drugs to ease
the pain. Margaret was born first. Mum says she probably organised that even in the womb—she's a bossy
little miss. Mikey was breech and he stuck in the birth
canal. Even with drugs, Katherine suffered.'

She looked out the window and, through a mist of
fresh tears, saw the sun strike the tops of the mountains.
Another birth—a brand-new day!

'She bought the house where we all live now, and

Mum and I came to live here with her. It's the twins' house now. It's held in trust for them.'

He wanted to say something but his throat had closed over so he reached out and touched her on the shoulder.

She turned to him and smiled.

'Heaven knows why I felt compelled to shed all that right now!' she muttered, embarrassment colouring her beautiful skin and darkening the lovely eyes. 'We all cry for Katherine sometimes, even the twins who don't really remember her, but I rarely thrust it onto total strangers.'

Her words shafted pain into his gut, stirring anger.

'Total strangers?' he asked coolly. First she falls asleep while I'm talking to her, and now she's cutting me out of her life again after we've shared a unique experience.

'Aren't we?' The colour deepened in her cheeks.

Again he cursed that kiss—yet not enough to prevent him wanting to stop the car and kiss her again.

'Neighbours would sound more friendly,' he pointed out, battling the absurd impulse.

'Neighbours! I'd looked forward to having neighbours.'

She spoke softly, a thought uttered aloud, but the words held an echoing regret—as if the reality hadn't matched her dreams.

Well, that was too bad! he thought crossly. What's more, he hadn't time to be neighbourly—he had a book to write.

A different book. . .

He glanced at her again. She was looking out of the window, watching as the sun's rays slid down the mountains—colouring them in as it went. She was disturbing, this woman, sneaking in under his guard at unexpected moments.

And she was danger—he knew that. An indefinable threat to his busy and usually well-ordered life. Yet if he wanted to do a different book—and the adrenalin surge every time he thought of it confirmed that he did—he would need her co-operation.

He considered how to tackle the subject as he drove and was startled by her muttered, 'Damn car!' as they reached the entrance to his drive.

'I'll take you down to the house,' he told her. 'Is there someone in town who'll come out to fix it?'

'Fix it or tow it away,' she said gloomily. 'Poor thing is on its last legs. I bought it second-hand when the twins were babies because Volvos are supposed to be the safest cars, but having to get around the countryside with my work has probably worn it out. . .'

Her long, drawn-out sigh filtered into his heart. She was too young and lovely to be bogged down with so much responsibility. He stopped outside her front door.

'It might be something simple wrong with it. You're tired at the moment and everything looks worse.'

She turned and smiled at him.

'You're right! I'm sorry. I don't usually lose it like this. And you've been so kind—I'd never have managed without you.'

It was a neat little speech but it angered him because she was setting him apart again—distancing herself from him as she had earlier.

Not that he cared!

'It was my pleasure,' he said stiffly and opened his door. 'I'll carry the bags inside for you.'

For a moment he thought she was going to argue, but she nodded abruptly and extricated herself from the car.

'Thanks again,' she repeated, standing in the entry as if to bar his admittance into the 'real' part of the house.

He said goodbye and left, annoyed by her sudden abruptness—and confused by the dismay it caused him.

Marnie watched him drive back up to the road, then turned wearily towards her bedroom. Thank heavens it was Saturday. The kids got up when they felt like it and fixed their own breakfast. With any luck, she wouldn't hear them and could sleep through until lunchtime. No classes today and no pre- or post-natal visits, although she'd go into town later and visit Anne and the twins.

A boy twin called Richard who'd be living in the valley long after her neighbour had headed back to the city. A child who'd remind her. . .

She went to sleep on the thought and woke to raised voices outside her window.

'Marnie says we should try to do things for ourselves. She says that it teaches us res-responsibility.'

He might have stumbled over the long word, but Mikey's voice was shrill with indignation.

She struggled to the window and peered blearily out into the unnecessarily bright morning.

Richard Cunningham was standing on her side of the hedge with what looked like an axe slung across one hefty shoulder. Mikey was glaring up at him while Margaret looked uneasily from one to the other.

'Where's your mother?' the man demanded as Marnie tried to make sense of the scene.

'She's asleep,' Margaret explained. 'And Pete's taken Gran and Kyle and Jill into town to do the shopping—'

'And Gran said we're to play quietly in or near the house until Marnie wakes up. Our side of the creek is near the house.'

The axe seemed to grow in sharpness and menace as

Marnie watched, and a sickness stirred inside her.

'What are you doing with my children and that axe?'
she demanded. 'What's going on?'

'I'm an axe murderer and I'm taking them down to
the creek—'

He flung the words at her in a tired, scratchy voice,
then stopped abruptly as if he'd realised he'd gone far
enough in front of the children.

Margaret wasn't too affected. In fact, she laughed and
moved closer to take his hand.

'Silly!' she said, smiling adoringly up into his face.

'We wanted to surprise you with the tree when you
woke up,' Mikey explained.

Going somewhere with this man and an axe was a
surprise for her? And what tree? Marnie shook her head
in an effort to clear her sleep-fogged brain. A tree! Of
course.

Mikey had been wanting to get their Christmas tree
set up. He'd been nagging about it for days.

She looked from the children to the axe on Richard's
shoulders, and felt embarrassment sweep over her.

'They had the axe?' she said faintly to Richard.

He nodded.

'I couldn't sleep and was sitting on my deck when I
glanced this way and saw these two heading down
towards the creek with this lethal weapon.'

He must have come through the tunnel in the bushes,
Marnie thought, seeing a small twig caught in his thick
darkness of his hair.

'And I yelled at you. I'm sorry.'

'You're always yelling at me,' he grumbled.

'We wanted to get the Christmas tree.' Mikey had
tired of the grown-up conversation and decided to

explain. 'You always say we should try to do things for ourselves before we ask for help.'

Marnie looked from the earnest face to the shining axe blade and her heartbeat accelerated. From the axe blade it was only a blink to Richard's face—a stony mask of disbelief.

'I didn't say that!' she stuttered. 'Well, I probably did, but Gareth Gordon said it first—though I'm sure he didn't mean with axes.'

The mask remained remote and cynical and she stumbled on.

'Gareth Gordon writes "how-to" books on bringing up children and most of his ideas are practical and sensible. . .'

One eyebrow rose, sending her into even more confusion.

'But of course he wouldn't have mentioned axes!' She decided it might be easier if she turned her attention to the twins.

'You know you shouldn't take tools without asking,' she said to Mikey.

'I told him that!' Margaret piped up righteously.

Marnie could feel Richard's eyes on her and wondered how much leg was showing beneath the oversized T-shirt she wore to bed. But she didn't have time to work out angles of sight—she had to sort out the children.

'You were still going along with Mikey's idea,' she told Margaret in a reproving voice, 'which is as bad as doing something wrong yourself. You know that!'

'Did Gareth Gordon tell you that as well?'

Richard's question diverted her attention back to him and she tugged at the hem of her T-shirt.

'No, he didn't,' she retorted. 'I do have some thoughts of my own.'

Why did she always end up arguing with the man? She breathed out carefully, took a fresh breath and then added more calmly, 'Thank you for coming to the rescue—again. If you leave the axe by that orange tree I'll take it back to the shed when I'm dressed.'

Thus calling attention to the T-shirt, you idiot! she added silently as his gaze strayed momentarily downwards.

'I'll put it away myself once we've cut down the tree young Mikey wants,' he said calmly. 'I can show him how to clean tools after using them. I suppose Gareth Gordon mentioned it as a good habit?'

She clamped her lips shut on a furious retort and watched him head towards the creek, the traitorous twins dancing by his side. Other friends teased her unmercifully about her reliance on her 'guru', as they called him, and she took their provocation with a smile. But one mention of the great man's name to this wretched new neighbour and he was bringing the revered doctor into every conversation.

Was Richard Cunningham also a medical writer? Was a book the project he had to finish? Was he perhaps less successful than Dr Gareth Gordon and his reaction to the man's name a show of professional jealousy?

She puzzled over it as she showered and dressed. Then she wondered if her neighbour had had any sleep. He'd certainly looked more alert than she felt.

He'd tried to sleep, but kept remembering the softness of the woman next door as she'd cried against his shoulder. Growing up with a sister had ensured his 'liberation', but he had to admit he'd felt all-powerful when she'd sought shelter in his arms.

'That's the tree we want!'

Mikey interrupted his thoughts and he stared in horror

at the full-grown she-oak the twins had decided would make the perfect Christmas tree.

'It's too big,' he said firmly, then recalled his own advice.

Don't dictate to children. Find a way to help them come to the correct conclusion.

If he couldn't remember his own words how could any over-extended parent hope to remember all the advice that he and other so-called experts thrust on them?

'I'm sorry,' he said, squatting down so that his face was on a level with the crestfallen Mikey's. 'I shouldn't have said that. It's a magnificent tree and I can see why you'd like to have it.'

'It's the best tree here and we wanted the best tree for Marnie,' Margaret told him, and he found himself in unexpected agreement with the thought.

'But will it fit through the door?' he asked. 'And if we do get it inside how do you think we could make it stand up without the big roots that hold it upright here on the creek bank?'

He saw Mikey thinking about this and knew he'd made up some lost ground.

'I wonder if we could perhaps find a smaller tree but do something with this one as well.'

Beneath them the creek chattered to itself, and in the branches above them he saw the brilliant blue flash of a kingfisher's wings.

'Something like decorate it here?' Mikey asked after a long, considering silence.

'I think so,' Richard replied.

'With streamers and fairy lights?' Margaret wanted details.

'Well, paper streamers will get wet if it rains and then fall apart, but perhaps we should have a look at the

neatly arranged and well-stocked garden shed. He shook his head.

'She must be superwoman.'

'Who?'

Margaret's demand told him he must have spoken the thought aloud. Again! Perhaps living in the country had been a mistake after all!

'Your mother—Marnie,' he explained. 'How does she find time to work, take care of four kids and use all these tools as well?'

'Oh, she doesn't do the garden,' Mikey told him. 'Pete does.'

His intestines went from mushy to knotted. Who the hell was Pete?

Perhaps he was an elderly gardener.

'How old is Pete?'

The question was out before he'd realised he was going to ask it. Thank heavens the older children weren't around to hear him making such a fool of himself! Margaret was eyeing him consideringly as it was.

'He's old,' she told him. 'Old as Marnie and you, I'd say.'

'Ask a stupid question. . .' he muttered under his breath as he checked that the axe was secure on its special hooks.

'I've been looking for you three.'

Marnie watched them emerge from the shed, Mikey carefully shutting and bolting the door behind them. She glanced towards Richard but avoided his eyes as memories of her angry accusations made her feel hot and uncomfortable.

'Morning tea's ready on the deck,' she said limply, and as the twins scampered away she had to look at Richard.

'Having prevented an almost certain limb or digit amputation, would you like to join us?' she added politely, although she knew that exposing herself to more of his company was akin to exposing her body to radium treatment. He had an unseen but destructive effect on her strength, not to mention her self-image which was crumbling a little more with each encounter.

'I'd enjoy that,' he said, joining her as she turned to follow the twins back to the house. 'What's happening with your car? I noticed it was gone from the top of the drive.'

It was a natural question in the circumstances but she found it difficult to answer him, as if her mind had taken a vacation unexpectedly. She dragged it determinedly into gear.

'It was loaded on a large truck and taken to town early this morning,' she explained. 'I won't know what's wrong until they have a look at it on Monday.'

'Monday?' he echoed, and she smiled at the surprise in his voice.

'You're in the country now,' she reminded him. 'Jack at the garage usually works Saturday mornings, but it's market day tomorrow and he makes the best chutney and pickles in the district. He shuts up shop and spends the day in the kitchen.'

She saw Richard shake his head and smiled at his disbelief.

'I can wait until Monday,' she assured him. 'Pete's home for the weekend so we're back to being a two-car family.'

He seemed to falter and, when she let her gaze slide sideways for a moment, she saw a darkness in his face.

'Perhaps I won't stay for morning tea,' he said

abruptly, and she stopped and turned to face him, hoping her dismay wasn't visible in her eyes.

'The children will be disappointed,' she said uncertainly.

'And you?' he growled. 'Would you be disappointed?'

She could feel the flush spread upward into her cheeks and wondered if they were flaming as hotly as she imagined.

'Yes, I would,' she said stiffly, 'but I realise you've probably wasted more time than you can afford on helping me and my family.'

She saw the play of emotion in the subtle movements of the muscles in his face. It fascinated her but gave her no indication of his thoughts. Then his grey eyes lightened to a silvery colour and he shrugged.

'It's not a matter of time!' The words were gruff but the smile accompanying them snagged at her heart, catching her unawares so that she had to hurry after him as he strode purposefully towards her house.

It was time he sorted this out, he told himself. Time he returned this woman to a box marked 'neighbour' in his mind! At the moment she was invading every crevice of it, and sexual fantasies he hadn't experienced since puberty were causing havoc in his body.

She caught up with him as they reached the front door, and led him through the house to where a wide verandah gave views across the valley.

His eyes found 'Pete' immediately—a tall rangy man with pitch black hair and dark eyes. He sat at ease in an old squatter's chair, with Jill perched on one arm of it and Kyle on the other.

Richard introduced himself formally to 'Gran'—Betty Ferguson—and brushed aside her thanks. Was he jealous because this Pete might be Marnie's lover, or jealous of his place in this family? And why, whichever way it went? The questions tormented him while he accepted a cup of tea—he'd be converted to tea-drinking if he stayed much longer in the country—and was ushered across the verandah to meet Pete.

Marnie hadn't followed him onto the verandah and Richard found himself waiting for her—listening for her footsteps in the house.

'The kids tell me you're a doctor. You starting a practice here or going in with the old fellow?' Pete asked.

Dragging his mind from thoughts of footsteps, Richard caught enough of the conversation to realise what Pete had asked.

'I'm a doctor but not here to practise—much to Marnie's disappointment. I've a written project I have to finish so I came down here to escape the chaos of life in the city.'

'Well, that's not a problem for me!' Pete drawled. 'I'm a mining engineer. Great job but it takes me into some fairly wild and remote country. I come back for some noise and company, don't I, kids?'

Jill nodded, and Kyle said excitedly, 'Pete's going to take me with him after Christmas. We're going to—'

He looked enquiringly at Pete.

'Irrawonga—far north-west of the state.'

Richard was pleased for the boy, but his uneasiness over this man's presence was growing with every word the family spoke. He'd been stupid to assume that Marnie Ferguson was unattached. An attractive, vibrant woman—of course she'd have a boyfriend. His mind balked at the word lover.

'Sorry, gang, I have to go!'

Marnie's voice made him spin around, and the

children's chorused 'Baby coming?' made him wonder just how often she was called out to work.

And reminded him of his idea!

'Could I drive you?' he asked, interrupting her request to borrow Pete's car. 'I'll explain why on the way.'

She hesitated, probably trying to think of a polite way to put him off.

'I'll get the car and be down at your front door by the time you've checked your bags,' he said, then strode away before she had time to argue.

'There was no need for you to do this,' she protested as they watched Kyle load the bags into the back of his vehicle.

'But I wanted to. As I said, I'll explain on the way. Hop in!'

He felt excited and in control again—and was honest enough to admit to himself that a good deal of his satisfaction came from knowing he'd taken her away from the enigmatic Pete.

'I thought of it last night,' he explained once she'd given him enough directions to get him started. 'I'm a writer and I'd been working on a book about parents and partners but it wasn't jelling.'

'Your project,' she said and he sensed satisfaction in her tone.

'My planned and contracted project!' he admitted. 'When I conceived the idea it seemed fine—a natural progression to my other work. Then last night, as I watched you deliver those two tiny babies, I wondered if if wasn't missing something far more important about children's lives.'

So he's a paediatrician, Marnie thought, uncertain whether she felt pleased or disappointed. He was still talking, and she tried to concentrate on his words.

'Until you said something about doctors taking over the actual delivery process. I began to wonder then how much work had been done on comparisons between home births and hospital deliveries.'

'Plenty, I would think,' she told him. 'Especially in England, where the tradition never died out. But didn't you say you were only here for a couple of months to meet a deadline? You can't write a book that's a study of home births in that time—think of the research you'd have to do. And the follow-up work—it's not just a matter of more placid babies. That's been quite well documented. What about comparisons of the children at different ages—other influences on their lives?'

She was excited by the thought, yet wary of the excitement. She glanced at him and thought about other kinds of excitement—

'I wasn't thinking of a scientific study.'

The flat statement slopped over her like a jug of cold water.

'Oh!'

Then he turned towards her and smiled, and a strange disturbance simmered again in her veins.

'I was thinking more of a collection of home-birth stories that might encourage other women to consider the possibility.'

'And encourage specialists and GPs to be more flex-ible in their thinking about it?' she queried, remembering the stories she'd heard from women who'd wanted to have their babies at home in other areas where a doctor's reaction might range from a flat 'no' to 'what a ridiculous idea'.

'Exactly!' he said, his smile broadening as he admit-ted, 'Although I can't guarantee I'd have any influence on fellow specialists!'

Marnie felt her mind whirling as she tried to pretend she wasn't affected by his smile.

'So that's why you're driving me.'

Disappointment nudged the happiness aside. She looked out at the rolling hills that softened the steepness of the mountains beyond them, choosing her words carefully.

'Last night was an emergency and I was pleased to have you there to help me. So was Anne! But a planned home birth is different. Childbirth's a very personal thing. The family know me from pre-natal visits. We've worked through the pregnancy together and planned the great moment for months.'

'And they won't want an outsider there?'

She nodded, uneasy and embarrassed.

'Well, it's a bit like someone coming along to watch a show, isn't it?' she muttered at him. 'Different if you'd met the family earlier. I could have pretended you were a trainee midwife.'

She smiled at the thought, but she was caught between a desire to help this man—or maybe to keep him by her side—and the sanctity of her patients' privacy.

Then he reached over and patted her on the arm.

'I had considered all of that,' he said softly. 'I'm not totally insensitive and I don't expect to be invited in today. But driving you was an opportunity to talk to you about it. To ask what you thought of the idea and if you'd mind if I tagged along on your rounds, spoke to those patients who were willing to meet me—that kind of thing.'

Her skin burnt beneath his touch and her thoughts simmered in the heat haze it generated.

'I can talk to my patients about it,' she said through lips as dry as chalk.

She realised she was committing herself to two months of his company in the close confines of a car—two months of having him watch her at work, of driving through the beautiful sun-splashed valleys with him and coming home in pearly dawns with him beside her. Of feeling him near her day and night. . .

CHAPTER SEVEN

MARNIE directed him towards the house hidden in the trees at the head of a narrow valley, relieved that the narrow road winding through the fern-littered rain forest demanded all of his attention.

'Harriet is an ex-teacher who now makes paper. Paul writes poetry. They've lived here for about seven years and this child will be their third.'

She explained this more to break the silence in the car than to provide him with information he probably wouldn't need. 'You can stop wherever you can find a space,' she added, staring with dismay at the collection of old trucks, vans, cars and bicycles cluttering the cleared area near the house.

As he cut the engine they could hear the muted sounds of revelry.

'I can see another person would be overdoing things!' Richard said, as a girl with flowers in her long flowing hair wafted past them and drifted along a track that led into the bush.

'Sometimes people invite their friends,' Marnie told him, aware of the stiffness in her voice.

'All their friends?' he persisted, his head cocked to one side as the noise from the house became a swelling cacophony of merriment.

'I'd better go and see what's happening,' Marnie muttered. 'I'll just take the small bag—Harriet will have all the sheets and towels we'll need.'

She climbed out of the car and looked back uncertainly at him.

'I don't mind waiting here,' he said, and smiled as if he meant it, but the words did little to alleviate her anxiety and the smile did nothing for her equilibrium.

'I'll come and tell you if it's likely to be a long wait,' she promised, then she grabbed her bag out of the back and hurried up towards the house.

He watched her stride away from him, seeing competence and certainty in her bearing. Yet she'd looked uneasy when she'd turned towards him, as if his presence was some new variable that didn't compute in the organised chaos of her life.

Then he saw her legs take the steps two at a time and he forgot about competence and confidence, thinking instead about the unpredictability of attraction and the dividing line between it and good old-fashioned lust.

Paul greeted Marnie at the top of the steps.

'I'm sorry about the chaos, but Harriet's pains began as the first guest arrived for Megan's birthday party. She thought she'd be able to manage until after it was over, but this one's in a hurry.'

Marnie sensed a tension in him, strange in someone as relaxed and laid-back as Paul.

'I'll get rid of them if you like,' she suggested. 'I'm sure they'd all understand.'

'Who?' he asked with a puzzled expression on his face.

'The party-people.' Marnie studied him more closely. He looked wretched, but not with the anxious look more common to expectant fathers. Paul's face reflected dread and sadness, and his preoccupation had nothing to do with the birthday party.

'What's wrong?'

He responded to the blunt question with a start, then shook his head.

'It might be nothing but these last few days Harriet hasn't felt any movement. She kept saying she felt different, as if something bad had happened.'

'Why didn't she call me?' Marnie demanded, and saw Paul shrug.

'She was busy organising the party, making it special. Having a birthday close to Christmas is hard enough on Megan, but with all the fuss over a new baby Harriet didn't want her to feel left out of things. And the baby wasn't due for a few weeks—'

'We had no real idea when the baby was due,' Marnie reminded him. 'She was at least three months pregnant before she realised it so we never had exact dates. We've been going on measurements, which is never as accurate with second or third babies.'

Another shrug.

'She wanted to handle it her way.'

'I'd better see her. Is she still at the party?'

Paul shook his head.

'She's in the bedroom. Do you think she'll be OK? Should we call Dr Crail?'

The last question underlined how worried Paul was. He believed in natural medicines and alternative treatments like massage for pain relief. Calling in a doctor was last-resort stuff!

'There's a doctor down in your car park if you feel you'd like him present. He's my new neighbour and he drove me because my car's packed up. I'll go up to Harriet—you decide.'

Marnie hurried into the house, avoiding the big front deck where the party was taking place and going directly to Harriet's and Paul's loft bedroom.

Harriet was propped against pillows on her bed, her face white and strained—wet by tears which seemed to flow endlessly down her cheeks.

'The baby's dead, I know it, Marnie,' she announced with a calmness that was more potent than hysteria. The high-pitched notes of children's laughter rose up from the deck and mocked her words.

'When did you feel a difference? Had something happened? Any bump or jolt? A show of blood?'

Marnie asked the questions as she listened for a foetal heartbeat. Let Harriet be wrong, she prayed. Let the baby be all right.

'It stopped kicking,' Harriet told her, 'about three or four days ago. I can't remember when because it might have been a day or two before I realised. I still felt movement, but it was more a bumping sensation than the feel of a kick.'

Marnie shifted her attention to Harriet, taking her blood pressure and then her pulse while she listened to the flat, matter-of-fact words which hid her heartache.

Throughout the examination Harriet's contractions continued, yet the woman seemed detached from what was happening in her body—as if grief had anaesthetised her more effectively than any drug.

'I'd say there's time to get to town. Would you prefer to go to hospital, perhaps deliver by Caesarean?'

Harriet shook her head.

'No. It's still my baby and I want to have it naturally— and to have it here in a place of beauty and happiness.'

She said the words with conviction, but there was another fear lurking behind them and Marnie waited, hoping that Harriet would eventually talk about what was worrying her.

She checked dilatation, timed contractions and quietly

prepared the room and the equipment she'd need. In one corner of the room she could see the carefully prepared crib, swathed in tie-dyed gauze so it looked like a magic grotto.

'We're into fairies here at the moment,' Harriet explained, seeing Marnie's interest. 'If you look down to the deck you'll see any number of them. Megan insisted—the baby—would—love it—'

For the first time the unnatural calmness cracked and Harriet's voice stumbled over the words.

'I should have had a scan!' she blurted out. 'Should have agreed to go up to Weldon and get it done when you suggested it.'

Marnie swallowed the lump in her throat and moved swiftly to the bed, sitting beside Harriet and drawing her body close.

'It would have told us the baby's gestational age, not that this would happen,' she assured her friend. 'If the baby has died the most likely cause is foetal abnormality of some kind. If the scan had picked that up the specialist would have suggested amniocentesis.'

'And I'd have refused that, too,' Harriet muttered. 'I've always been a great believer in foetal rights and non-invasive tests and treatments.'

Marnie heard the bitter taint of guilt in Harriet's words and spoke swiftly.

'Harriet, I know you and I know Paul. I helped you bring Joey into the world. I've seen you rearrange furniture in your kitchen so you wouldn't disturb a spider's web in one corner. Think sensibly now. If a scan or a test had shown an abnormality would you have had the pregnancy terminated?'

Harriet looked at her, then out towards the tree-tops surrounding her bedroom. Marnie waited, knowing that it was important for Harriet to think this question through.

'I'd have talked to Paul,' she whispered, and at that moment Paul's head appeared on the stairway.

'He's here now,' Marnie pointed out, waving Paul forward while she signalled to Richard to stay out of the way. 'Talk to him now. Shall I ask him the same question?'

Harriet nodded and Marnie moved so that Paul could take her place beside his wife.

'Harriet's fretting because she chose not to have tests earlier in the pregnancy. We did all the usual things like testing for diabetes and anaemia, but no scans, no amniocentesis. I've just asked her if you would have decided to terminate the pregnancy if she'd had the tests and we'd found an abnormality.'

'You mean abort the baby? No way!'

Marnie smiled in spite of her concern. Paul hadn't needed to consider it for an instant.

'You know we wouldn't have done that, love,' he said to his wife. 'Couldn't have done that!'

Harriet sighed and nestled against him. 'So having the tests would have made no difference to this moment?'

She asked Paul but looked at Marnie.

'None!' she said. 'Although, perhaps, if we'd picked up an abnormality you'd have had time to consider possible outcomes.'

She knew she'd have to question her own convictions later—have to think through her code that women should have the last say in regard to what was happening with and to their bodies.

'I'd have rather not have known,' Harriet said slowly. 'Paul and I have talked about cancer diagnosis and we don't like the thought of someone putting a limit on our lives. But there's Megan and Joey. . .'

She broke off suddenly, breath snatched from the words as the desire to push overcame her. Her waters burst, too much water, Marnie realised as she concentrated on her job. Paul must have waved Richard into the room for she heard introductions and sensed his presence beside her.

Harriet grunted and the uterus widened, moving swiftly through the stages of an oval aperture to crowning, then the lifeless form slid into the world.

'It's anencephaly,' she said quietly, wiping the tiny distorted features and wrapping the little female form closely in a soft towel. 'It's a condition where the brain and spinal cord don't develop normally. She wouldn't have lived long if she'd been born alive, Harriet. Perhaps it's better this way.'

She was aware of Richard beside her, clamping and cutting the cord while she cradled the still infant in her arms.

Her voice was strained as she held back tears of shock and pity.

'All we could have done was kept her warm and comfortable.'

She thought of the fairy crib and swallowed hard, knowing there was more that had to be said.

'Do you want to see her—to hold her?' she asked. 'The malformation means she looks different. . .'

She faltered and felt Richard's arm around her shoulders, exerting an oh-so-comforting pressure.

'We'd like to hold her, then we'd like to put her in the crib. The children should have the opportunity to say goodbye to her.'

It was Paul who spoke, but Harriet who reached out for the baby.

Marnie passed her over, and concentrated on the delivery of the placenta. The sooner she could tidy up and leave these two to mourn the better. She set aside her own shock and sadness, concentrating fiercely on practicalities.

'Is someone staying to help Paul look after you and the children?' she asked Harriet.

'Mum's here,' Harriet replied, turning to watch as Paul put the swaddled infant in the crib. 'She's keeping the fairies in order downstairs.'

'I'll go down and see her when I've finished,' Marnie promised. She examined the placenta and slid it into a plastic bowl she carried for this purpose. Some families wanted the placenta buried near their home, but most left its disposal to Marnie.

'I'll bury it near Joey's,' Paul said quietly and she nodded. This child was just as real to them as the two who had lived. She snapped the lid on the bowl and set it aside, knowing it would be part of Paul's mourning process to do this for his daughter.

She worked swiftly, gently sponging and dressing Harriet to leave her clean and comfortable. Below them music played, but the childish shrieks and laughter had died away.

'Would you like a drink? Something to eat?' she asked Harriet as she packed her bag.

'Perhaps later,' Harriet said. 'First we'd better see Mum and the kids.'

Her face was grey with grief and strain.

'Shall I tell them?' Marnie asked, dreading the task yet hoping to spare Harriet more trauma.

'I'd told Mum I was worried. I guess that's why she's

shuffled the party guests out of the way.' She looked at Paul, who took over for her.

'We have to tell the kids ourselves,' he said, then hesitated, looking from Marnie to Richard. 'But would you mind waiting? Make yourselves a cup of tea or coffee; forage for something to eat. There are things I'd like to ask you—to talk to you about.'

Like funerals, Marnie realised, and possibly genetics if you're thinking further ahead.

Richard took her bag and led the way down the steep staircase. He waited at the bottom, reaching out a hand to steady her.

'Are you OK?' he asked, and the sympathy in his voice all but undid her.

'I'll manage,' she told him, smiling through the tears that had filled her eyes. 'Harriet's mother, Mrs Benson, will be in the kitchen.'

A clattering noise from beyond the huge stone fire-place told her she'd guessed correctly. With Richard by her side, she walked reluctantly towards the sounds of activity.

'No good?'

The middle-aged woman looked up as they entered, She was washing dishes, her arms sheathed in soap-suds.

Marnie shook her head.

'It's a little girl—stillborn,' she said softly, and saw the older woman bow her head. 'Harriet and Paul would like to see you and the children.'

'They're on the verandah, playing with Megan's new bubble pipe.' Mrs Benson nodded towards the open glass doors. 'Would you send them up? I'll follow in a moment.' She fumbled in her pocket and Marnie caught the sheen of tears on her eyelashes.

Marnie walked slowly towards the verandah, where

swirls of rising bubbles caught the sun, breaking its light into rainbow colours.

'As beautiful and fragile as life itself,' Richard murmured, coming to stand behind her as she reached out and let a bubble settle on the palm of her hand.

'As transient as happiness?' she asked, looking towards the laughing, excited children. Megan was in her fairy dress, translucent wings shimmering with patterns of gold and silver glitter. Joey had probably started the afternoon as an elf for tatters of green crêpe paper still clung to his T-shirt and a tiny green cap was perched askew over one eye. Marnie's heart clenched with pain for them.

Richard touched her arm.

'Happiness can be recaptured, rebuilt into a new and different emotion, maybe, but still a welling-up of joy.'

And as he spoke she watched Megan dip her bubble wand in the soapy liquid and draw it through the air so that a bright chain of bubbles arced above her head.

'Your mum and dad would like to see you both in the bedroom,' Marnie said, as the glittering spheres drifted into the surrounding bush.

The children turned to her, their eyes wary, then hand in hand they slipped across the verandah and into the house.

Marnie crossed the deck and peered out into the myriad greens of the rain forest. Richard came and stood beside her, and when he put his arm around her shoulders and drew her close she found the contact so comforting that she wanted to rest her head against him—to snuggle up to his warmth and let him carry some of the load she was burdened with today.

Common sense warned that this might not be a good idea. Particularly the snuggling up part as her body, depressed though it was by the recent tragedy, was still overly receptive to subconscious signals from his. At least she hoped they were subconscious.

'Kids can cope with most traumas providing they have kind and loving support,' he offered.

'I suppose so!'

'You don't sound convinced. Doesn't Gareth Gordon tell you that in one of his books?' He spoke in a light, teasing murmur that made her skin prickle with awareness.

'I think he does. In fact, I know he does. I keep reading that bit to try to convince myself. It's not that I don't believe you, or him, or any other expert,' she told him, shifting restlessly from one foot to the other but not moving away from the light clasp of his arm. 'I just hate the fact that kids should have to deal with this stuff. I know they can, and that through the experience they will probably learn to handle trauma later on but. . .'

'But you'd prefer to shield them from it—to provide a perfect childhood as unrealistic as a perfect world.'

The cynicism she suspected in the words made her angry.

'Well, I had a perfect childhood! I had parents and grandparents and a sister and brother and pets and friends, and no one who molested me or beat me or left me at home at night on my own. . . And the babies I knew didn't die!'

She heard a note of desperation in her voice and ducked away from Richard before he felt her pain.

'I suppose that's why I grew up argumentative and hysterical,' she added, hoping the flippant remark might divert his attention from her more passionate outburst. Of course, he could win this argument by pointing out that if she'd had to handle grief when she was younger she might be handling this situation better right now.

'I agree with you,' he said, moving so he was close again, but not touching her. 'I think a happy childhood is the most precious gift parents can give their children. But death is so much part of life that we have to accept it some time. I'm sure you faced it as a child—death of a grandparent, death of a pet—but because you had loving parents it became part of the mosaic of your youth, a few tiles of a deeper colour maybe, not a great gaping black hole where a huge fistful of happiness was torn out.'

Marnie smiled at the metaphor as she considered his words.

'You're right,' she admitted. 'Actually, Gareth Gordon sometimes talks about a mosaic of life.' Her smile became a slightly embarrassed grin. 'I know you probably think I'm crazy quoting this paediatrician all the time but he writes such sensible, useful books. I could never have raised the twins or coped with Kyle and Jill without him.'

Coped with Kyle and Jill? The words rang in Richard's mind, disrupting the feeling of pleasure her innocent praise had provided.

'I don't think you're crazy at all. Surely the more we read and learn about any subject the better we'll understand it.'

He gave an inward groan as he realised how unutterably stuffy he sounded! He glanced towards Marnie, but she'd turned away. The slim shape of her body and the dark russet of her hair were clearly defined against the green of a lacy tree fern. He had to battle an impulse to rest his hands on her hips—to step up behind her and press his body against hers.

'I suppose your projects are far more scientific,' she muttered.

He reached out to touch her, wanting to tell her—to have her turn to him and smile with delight—but she hadn't finished, and her next words left his hand hanging foolishly in the air.

'And Gareth Gordon probably seems hopelessly old-fashioned to you.' She spun around and he could see a smudge of dampness across one cheek as if she'd brushed away a tear. Then she smiled, and he almost missed what she was saying as he felt a thudding in his chest and a thunderous rush of blood in his ears.

'I picture him as a grandfatherly figure,' she confided. 'I know he's only recently found popularity with his books and newspaper columns, but I imagine him a bit like Dr Crail—a man who's retired while his brain was still sharp—sitting in some book-lined study and passing on his accumulation of knowledge and wisdom to parents all over the world.'

If he hadn't been having some kind of heart attack he'd have been mortified, but he was too caught up in his body's peculiar behaviour to equate the white-haired old gent with himself.

'Marnie, Harriet would like to talk to you.'

Mrs Benson's voice startled him, but Marnie must have been expecting it. She crossed the deck so swiftly that he had the impression she was eager to escape.

From what? His company?

Now that was a depressing conclusion.

'Like a cup?'

He'd missed the rest of Mrs Benson's sentence. He assumed she was offering tea or coffee and assented politely.

'Perhaps I can help?' he added, walking back into the house.

Mrs Benson seemed more pleased to have company than assistance, chatting to him as she bustled around the kitchen setting out cups and saucers, preparing a tray to carry upstairs and opening tins of cakes and biscuits.

'I did a lot of baking because Paul was to be at home to take care of Harriet and I'd wanted to leave them on their own for a while. When Joey was born the party seemed to go on for days, with people staying over and others dropping in. Harriet was enjoying it, but she didn't realise how tiring it was—and Joey was cranky because her milk hadn't come in properly and he wasn't getting enough to eat. In the end Marnie came and turfed us all out, then put a "No Visitors" sign on the front gate until they'd had time to settle into being a family again.'

He was picturing Marnie in this role when Mrs Benson continued.

'Do you think I should still go home, or should I stay on with them?'

He saw the worry in her eyes—and the sadness. She wanted to do the right thing but if she left she'd have to grieve alone.

'If you feel you'd like to stay tell Harriet and Paul. I think they'll understand it's a time for all the family to be together.'

She seemed relieved and her fingers shook a little as she put biscuits on a plate, then lifted the tray to take upstairs.

'The tea's in the pot,' she told him. 'And that sounds like Marnie coming back down. Pour her a cup—she probably needs it.'

The slim legs came into view first, attention-riveting in their shapeliness. Then shorts, a neat waist, a dark green T-shirt and finally the complete picture, her lips curving into a warm smile as she stepped aside to let Mrs Benson go up the stairs.

Richard felt the tightening in his chest—again—and tried to concentrate on pouring tea. He found milk in the refrigerator and added it to his cup, grimacing as he looked at the watery brew.

'Is that tea?' Marnie asked, crossing the big room with the swift stride he found characteristic of her. 'What a blessing!'

She looked up at him, her lovely eyes untroubled now. Healing must have begun in the bedroom loft.

'Do you want milk?' he stuttered, waving the small jug towards her. For one paralysing moment another question had nearly popped out, though why 'Will you marry me?' was suddenly hammering in his head he didn't know. As she'd said only yesterday, they were total strangers. Well, virtual strangers! And then there was the little matter of the four children—and his ambivalence towards children as a species!

She shook her head and lifted the cup of pale liquid to her lips, sipping delicately.

Pretending composure, he mirrored her movements, but the first sip was enough make him choke and gag. He all but dropped the cup back on to the bench.

'That's not tea!' he protested, running water into a glass to get rid of the cloying unfamiliar taste.

Her laughter rippled out at first, then expanded into a rich melodious burst of amusement.

'It's not funny!' he snapped, 'I admit I'm not a tea-drinker, but that was dreadful!'

Her amusement simmered down to a few smothered chuckles, but as she raised her cup again he reached out to grasp her hand.

'Don't drink it,' he urged. 'There's something wrong.'

Ignoring him completely, she sipped again—consideringly this time—then swallowed with every sign of enjoyment.

'Maybe it's the milk I put in it,' he muttered, aware that he had managed to make a complete idiot of himself.

'Or maybe raspberry leaf tea hasn't come your way before,' she suggested with a smile that drew him into the joke.

'Raspberry leaf tea? People make tea out of raspberry leaves?'

'And many other garden plants, herbs especially.'

He nodded and found himself smiling back at her.

'I guess I always knew that,' he admitted. 'I just didn't know people drank the stuff!'

'If you're serious about wanting to be part of some home births while you're in the district you'll soon realise the hills around Clareville are practically a caffeine-free zone. If you're addicted you'll have to carry your own supply.'

He looked out at the tree-tops beyond the deck and wondered if tranquillity and natural beauty might prove more addictive than caffeine—and Marnie Ferguson more addictive than opium!

'I don't think I'm an addict but I guess that remains to be seen. I'd like to see more of your service while I'm here but you and your patients must have the final say in that.'

Movement drew his gaze back to her. She rinsed her cup, dried it carefully, folded the teatowel over a rack and put the cup in the cupboard—then finally turned to face him.

'I spoke to Paul and Harriet about your wanting to accompany me.' She met his eyes with a directness he found disconcerting until he saw shadows in the darkness and wondered if, beneath her determination to be fair, she was troubled by the idea. 'They feel other families would accept your presence. . .' She hesitated. 'But perhaps that's because they were so pleased to find a doctor was on hand.'

'I couldn't have done anything—no doctor could,' he assured her, realising that her friends' reaction to her question may have undermined her confidence.

'I know that!' she retorted. 'Not in this case. But I can't help thinking how great it would be if we could attract the right doctor to the area. Someone who is positive about home birth, someone to work with me. He could take over all the pregnancies from Dr Crail, who could still practise part-time and see people when the new doctor was called out. We'd be a team, he and I. . .'

Richard's intestines knotted at the 'he and I' bit. The shadows had disappeared from Marnie Ferguson's eyes and she was smiling blissfully at her dream, oblivious of his presence. He hadn't even started doing rounds with her, and already she had him replaced by some virtuous paragon of a GP.

'And no doubt he'll be tall, dark and handsome, single, of course, and madly fond of children,' he growled. 'I'll wait in the car.'

He stormed away, aware that he'd made a complete and utter idiot of himself.

CHAPTER EIGHT

MARNIE watched him leave, frowning over the unexpected outburst. Why was Richard so upset and what did the age, sex, looks, likes and dislikes of a new GP have to do with him? He'd already said he wasn't staying.

She phoned Dr Crail who would have to issue a death certificate and Cec Williams, the local undertaker, to ask him to come out and speak to Harriet and Paul. It was all she could do, she realised, as she collected her bag from the bottom of the steps, called a goodbye up the stairs and headed for the car.

Richard wasn't there. She left her bag beside it and crossed the now-deserted clearing towards the narrow track the flower child had taken earlier. The forest closed around her—damp, intensely green and secretive. Ahead, she heard the splash of water and she remembered that her creek rose in the mountains above this house.

He was standing by a natural rock pool, filled by water cascading down over a ledge of rocks.

'I hadn't realised people could live so close to nature that they have their own waterfall not twenty feet from their home.'

'It's a special delight,' Marnie agreed.

'And that path?'

Richard pointed to where the track gave way to stepping stones beyond the pool, then began again on the far side of the creek.

'It leads to two other houses, tucked away in the rain

forest. They would be ten kilometres apart by road, but only ten minutes' walk along the track.'

'Close but not too close,' he said.

'More what you were looking for when you wanted a quiet place in the country—neighbours you couldn't see or hear?'

He turned to face her and his eyes were the opaque silver of mercury. He seemed to hesitate, studying her intently, then he smiled with a suddenness that flooded her body with joy.

'It might have been, but I wouldn't swap my new neighbours for a dozen waterfalls.'

Did he move, or did she?

She thought about it—a long time later—but couldn't decide. All she remembered was the pressure of his hands on her shoulders, then sliding across her back— enfolding her in a warm and comforting hug which lasted a whole nanosecond before it turned to a kiss of such hunger that she felt the aftershocks of it rippling through her toes.

Her response was as urgent as it was unexpected. Her lips touched his and parted with a soundless sigh. Her body pressed closer and moulded itself to his, seeking its own solace, but it was the feel of his mouth on hers, the tangle of their tongues, that sparked a fiery longing in her blood and made her pulses throb with a wanton desire.

His hands moved, a gentle exploration of her body, starting aches in nerve centres she'd never felt before, tightening her skin with wanting—filling her to bursting with a need she couldn't understand.

Her fingers gripped his hair, his head, holding him close while his mouth explored her cheeks, her jaw, the little hollow below her ear. . .

She heard her own gasp of pleasure-pain and his throaty chuckle, then he was kissing her again, more gently this time, kisses full of sweetness and tenderness and promises of treats in store.

'We'd better go,' he said at last, his arms once again embracing her in what could have been a neighbourly hug.

'I suppose so,' she muttered, standing limply in his arms while wave after wave of embarrassment washed over her.

Then the short call and answering whip-like crack of two whip-birds startled her into action. She stepped out of his encircling arms and headed back along the track, moving swiftly from a threat more potentially painful than the lash of a real whip.

He joined her in the car, started the engine and drove slowly back on to the narrow road. He didn't glance her way, or touch her, or ask directions—just drove.

The silence between them grew in weight and awkwardness until Marnie feared it would explode. She considered small-talk but it seemed so inappropriate after the sadness they'd left behind them. She wondered about medicine—after all, it was the one thing they had in common—but most of her medical knowledge seemed to have shifted to another part of her brain and she couldn't dredge up a satisfactory topic.

So she let the silence linger for a few more minutes, then heard her lips put into words her most pressing thoughts.

'I don't do a lot of kissing,' she blurted out, then turned, overwhelmed by embarrassment, and stared intently out the window.

Richard glanced her way and saw the hot colour in her cheeks. It made him want to stop the car and take her in his arms again but he, though equally confused, knew exactly where even the most neighbourly of embraces would lead. His body was throbbing with a passion he'd never experienced before, as if this red-haired woman he barely knew had possessed him in some way.

'I don't do much myself these days,' he found himself admitting.

Then he sighed. He'd said it hoping to ease her embarrassment, but consideration told him it was true. Maybe that was the problem! Maybe it had been too long since he'd had a light-hearted affair with some friend or colleague who shared his lack of interest in a permanent attachment.

Marnie heard his words but continued to study the surroundings as if they were as foreign to her as the landscape of Mars. What was happening to her? Why did this man affect her this way? Had some wanton genetic streak in her suddenly come to life in her body?

She shook her head, smiling at the idea of a rampant promiscuous gene travelling down from either of her parents.

'I could do with a laugh if you want to share that thought.'

She turned at the sound of his voice, the smile lingering on her lips.

'I was trying to blame genetics,' she admitted, 'but after serious consideration of my parents, who were so devoted to each other they didn't spend a night apart throughout their marriage, I think I'd better stick to some hormonal imbalance as an excuse.'

She spoke lightly, hoping she might be able to pass her reaction off as a joke.

'Do you need an excuse?' he asked. 'And do you feel

you need to justify your reaction to yourself or to me? We kissed, Marnie, and it was good. Can't it stand alone as something that happened, without analysis or explanations?'

She stared at him, unable to believe he could be serious.

Of course he could, her practical self told her. Your response was probably standard stuff for a worldly man like Richard Cunningham.

How depressing!

She studied the profile offered to her view, the clean line of his nose, the full curve of his lips and the slight tilt to his jaw which could suggest a stubborn streak.

Could he be stubborn? Would she have the opportunity to find out?

Heat flared in hidden recesses of her body, the idea of opportunities firing autonomic nerves to action.

'It's ridiculous!' she muttered to herself, as Richard turned onto the road that led to both their homes.

'Too ridiculous to try again?' he asked, slowing the car and guiding it towards an opening in a grove of trees.

Her heart pounded with excitement, squeezing the air out of her lungs so the 'yes' she should have said was never uttered.

'Maybe it was just a one-off thing, and you won't react at all a second time,' he suggested, and she saw the laughter lurking in his eyes and plucking at the corners of his lips.

Then his mouth closed over hers and she knew he was wrong, knew it as her hands moved against his chest, finding rapid heartbeats that matched the galloping rhythm of her own. She could feel her body weakening, stimulated against her will—and all common sense—as it welcomed his touch, the feel of his warmth, the texture of his skin.

Then once again his mouth moved, his tongue tasting her as kisses brushed her temple, cheek and neck. She tensed, wanting and not wanting more, desire a fiery burning in her skin. One hand touched her breast, one finger lingering against her nipple—shooting sparks along unseen pathways until she groaned with a hunger beyond her understanding.

The teasing finger stopped, his hand drew her head around so that his lips caught the remnants of the sound. He seemed to drink from her, draining her strength, her will, but when the questing fingers brushed against her nipple the quiver of delight made her jerk away from him.

'It's ridiculous!' she repeated, pressing her hands against cheeks that had to be glowing red they felt so hot. 'Impossible!'

She felt his hand on her hair, stroking gently.

'Why?' he murmured. 'It's not illegal or immoral, Marnie.'

His voice seduced her as effectively as his hands and lips, and she felt the treacherous weakening begin again.

'Just impractical,' she pointed out, turning to face him so he could see the regret she felt. 'In case it's escaped your notice, my house is full of mothers and kids, including a teenager who's facing his own hormonal uncertainties. I can hardly have you sleeping over at my place when I'm trying to teach my kids responsible sexual behaviour, and I don't think I'm desperate enough to go sneaking over to your place in the middle of the night.'

He frowned at her, his dark brows gathering and little creases showing in his forehead.

'Why are you so determined to label this as purely sexual?' he grumbled. 'Why put our feelings down to lust and make the whole thing something shameful?'

Her heart thundered with totally irrational hope, but she ignored such stupidity and met his eyes with a stout defiance.

'What else could it be?' she demanded. 'We barely know each other so it's unlikely to be love!'

It would have sounded OK if she hadn't stumbled on the final word and blushed again as her temerity in saying such a thing overcame her.

'No,' he responded gravely. 'It's unlikely to be love.'

He watched the colour fluctuate in her cheeks, and considered what else it might be as he started the car again and reversed carefully out onto the road.

It might be a virus of some kind, his helpful medical brain suggested. Something simple and life-threatening like myocarditis which affected the muscles of the heart and would explain that organ's recent unruly behaviour. Or natural male-female chemistry, the reaction more potent because of his recent celibacy.

And she was right! It *was* ridiculous. One glance at the woman was enough to tell him that she wasn't the type for a light-hearted affair and anything else, as far as he was concerned, was out of the question. Quite apart from the fact that he wasn't the marrying kind, there was a little matter of four children. He might be good with the theoretical stuff about children, but what man in his right mind would take on four?

'Perhaps your coming with me on my rounds isn't a good idea,' she announced as he came up the hill towards the entrance to her drive.

Disappointment was bitter on his tongue, but he'd never given up without a fight.

'Not even if a practical book about home birth makes it easier and more acceptable for women to choose that option? It might even encourage more medicos to consider it a viable option and you could find keen-eyed doctors flocking to your valley as they flocked in the eighties to Pithiviers in France to learn about underwater birth.'

It was an unfair tactic because he knew how passionate she was about her work. Passionate enough to set aside her concerns over their attraction to each other?

He could almost hear her thinking, and found it difficult to breathe while he waited for her reply. It came on the heels of a long, drawn-out sigh.

'I'm doing a home visit to check out a house for suitability for a home birth on Monday.'

He heard the words, light and clear—and the deep undertones which belied the carefreeness she tried to project. He noticed her fingers, clasped so tightly in her lap that the knuckles gleamed through her skin. He felt guilty that he'd forced this decision on her, but he had two imperatives now—a new book, and an excuse to see more of this woman. Seeing more of her would be a sure cure for whatever ailed him.

Wouldn't it?

He thrust the unwelcome doubt aside and thought about the new book.

'Would I be welcome?'

'I can ask,' she told him. 'I can't see why they'd object as it is only a home visit and it will give you some idea of the preparations we have to make.'

Her fingers seemed to relax slightly and he decided to keep the conversation going. Some protective instinct had been prodded into life and he found he didn't want the attraction between them to become another burden for her.

'Preparations?' he repeated.

She turned towards him and he saw a brave replica of her normal lovely smile.

'You'll see,' she promised. 'Just approach the outing with an open mind and be prepared to think before you speak.'

The smile had become more natural, beguiling him into thinking. . .

'Are you accusing me of rashness in my actions?'

And now she laughed, the notes as clear as the bell-birds' he'd heard in the forest earlier.

'One kiss might be impulse,' she reminded him. 'The second was a definite indication of rashness.'

His heart went into its two-step routine again, but he held it in check.

'Actually,' he murmured, sliding his gaze towards her to wait for her reaction, 'I remember three.'

She coloured as he'd known she would, and he had to grip the steering-wheel with all his might to prevent his hand from reaching out to feel the heat beneath that clear, betraying skin.

'Well, three's a good number,' she told him as he swung the car into her drive. 'Let's stop at three.'

He pulled up outside her door and turned towards her. Her eyes begged him to agree, but his body ached to hold her one more time. Then he heard the muted shouts of the children and knew they wouldn't be alone for long.

'If that's what you want we'll stop at three,' he growled. 'For the moment!'

And why he'd added that, he couldn't think.

Richard shoved open the door and climbed out to carry her bags into the house. Then Pete appeared, taking them from his hands with a casual, 'Thanks, mate,' and he knew he had to get away before a primitive urge to punch the man overcame him.

Marnie watched from the entry as the car whipped up the drive.

'Trouble, little sister?'

Pete's voice made her turn but she found she couldn't answer—couldn't tell him that a baby was dead and Richard Cunningham had kissed her and she was so mixed up she didn't know if she'd ever work her way back to normality.

'Your new neighbour bothering you?'

He *was* bothering her. Bother with a capital B, but not in a way she could discuss with her brother.

And her own feelings were of even more concern.

'I know you love the kids and would do anything for them, but you're entitled to a life of your own, Marnie,' he persisted.

She smiled at Pete.

'Sure!' she joked. 'Movies with the girls on Thursdays, Friday and Saturday nights out with the boy-friend—that's if I could find one who'd take on me and four kids!'

She stared up the drive again.

'I don't want that, Pete. It doesn't interest me and I don't feel I'm missing out on anything.'

'So what's the problem? Tell me!'

Not one to give in lightly, her brother!

'Oh, I suppose it *is* that irritating man!' she admitted, shrugging one shoulder as if the irritation were physical. 'First he shifts in next door and yells at the kids, then he refuses to help out Dr Crail and now he wants to come on my rounds with me.'

'To help you?' Pete enquired, his voice puzzled, probably by her vehemence.

'No!' she retorted. 'For his own selfish ends.'

She explained about the book, admitting, 'Well, eventually it might be good for a lot of people, but. . .'

'But you don't want him tagging along?'

The answer should have been a definite negative, but now the question had been asked she found she couldn't say the word.

'I've got to empty my bag and re-pack it,' she said instead. She picked up the smaller bag and headed for her bedroom where her medical supplies and sterile equipment were kept in a locked cupboard.

'I'm taking Mum and the kids up to the national park,' Pete called after her. 'I thought we'd walk the gully track. Do you want to come or would you prefer to rest?'

'I'll stay at home,' she told him. 'I've a heap of book-work to do and some phone calls to make.'

'Asking permission to bring the irritating man on your visits?' Pete teased, and something in his voice made Marnie turn back to look at him.

He walked up to her and gave her a hug.

'Don't be afraid of your feelings, love,' he said gently. 'And don't use the kids as an excuse to hide from the normal experiences of life.'

Then he kissed her on the top of her head and walked away, leaving her staring down the passageway at his retreating back.

Normal experiences of life? Was he talking about sex? About her having an affair? Or was she so caught up in her own knots of emotion that she was putting a physical connotation to his words?

She shook her head and continued into the bedroom, dumped her bag, then went out to say goodbye. Perhaps if she had a sleep her world would have reverted to normal by the time she woke, and the sizzling uncertainties in her body would have died away. And she wouldn't give her neighbour a passing thought.

It worked, after a fashion, until Sunday evening! She was in the kitchen preparing salads for a barbeque dinner on the deck when she heard his voice and the children greeting him with loud cries of welcome.

She strained her ears to hear more, but the children's conversation had dropped to a murmur—which was odd in itself. The twins, in particular, were more likely to trumpet their knowledge and wishes to the world at large. They'd been to the markets with Jim. Were they telling him about the treat he had in store next weekend?

Perhaps he wouldn't come in, she thought, then couldn't decide if she'd be pleased or disappointed.

'I called down to ask if you'd contacted the family you're visiting tomorrow.'

Now he'd sneaked into the kitchen without her hearing him!

And he'd come on business!

'Whatever happened to, "Hello, how are you today?"' she muttered, turning in time to see him edge uncertainly closer.

Or was she imagining the uncertainty?

'I thought you favoured a strict, businesslike approach,' he complained. 'I could go out and come in again. I did have the "hello" part all ready when I came down the drive but by the time I'd run the gauntlet of the kids. . .'

She stared at him. It *was* uncertainty! Here was this big-city, man-of-the-world, presumably experienced male as ill-at-ease as she was. Or was it a sham—an act to make her trust him?

'Where's Pete?'

The switch in conversation made her blink, and the aggravation in his voice unsettled her further. But at least Pete was a neutral topic.

'He's gone over to the coast to surf all day and hang around noisy bars at night. Says he gets enough peace and quiet on the job.'

'That's hardly fair on you,' Richard protested, stepping closer so she had to back away to keep a reasonable amount of air-space between them.

'Why?' she demanded, leaping to the defence of her brother. 'Because of the kids? They're hardly his responsibility. He's actually much better than most uncles, making sure he spends time with them—arranging to take Kyle back with him after Christmas.'

'Real uncle?' Richard asked suspiciously.

'What do you mean, "real uncle"?' Marnie glared at him, refusing to be distracted by the glint of grey eyes beneath straight dark lashes.

'I mean it's often a courtesy title children give to their mother's male "friends",' he said curtly, his grey eyes flashing sparks.

'Don't you mean lovers?' she snapped as comprehension struck her with the force of a mild cyclone. 'Isn't that what you mean? And what kind of a person does that make me, in your lofty estimation?' she demanded. 'A loose female who'd kiss any man who happened to be around even while her boyfriend was waiting at home?'

'Who's kissing any man? And who's got a boyfriend waiting at home? Did you ask Richard to stay to dinner? Kyle told him you probably would.'

Marnie gazed at Margaret, speechless with dismay

that she'd lost her temper with this man—again—and had done it where the children could have heard every word.

And the kids expected her to ask him to dine with them!

'It's all too much!' she muttered, and flung her hands up in the air.

'I'm a dab hand at a barbeque,' Richard offered as she turned away to finish the salads.

Marnie sighed, her anger dissolving as swiftly as it had risen.

'Ask him if he'd like to stay to dinner, Margaret,' she said in a resigned voice, 'then show him where the barbeque is. It's time it was lit.'

She heard Margaret's excited, 'You will stay, won't you, Mr Cunningham?' and Richard's deep assent. She heard movement and thought they'd gone, but then he was standing behind her, touching her gently on the shoulder.

'I think you're something very special,' he said quietly, then he turned her so that she could see his face, his tender smile. 'And "loose female" would be the last expression I'd use about you!'

He tapped his forefinger lightly on her nose.

'Now I'll light your barbeque!' he said, and walked away, leaving her more confused than ever.

Thankfully, her mother bustled in at that stage, fresh from a sleep and bath and ready to take over the supervisory role in the kitchen.

'Why don't you get yourself a drink and go and sit on the deck?' she said to Marnie. 'Send Kyle and Jill in to carry the plates and salad. What will you have? A glass of wine? You could pour one for me while you're at it.'

Marnie heard the words but remained where she was, staring out of the window towards the gas-fired barbeque and the man who squatted in front of it while two small red-headed children excitedly pointed out the different knobs and buttons.

'Oh, Richard's here, is he?' Her mother came to stand beside her. 'Perhaps he'd prefer a beer. I think Pete left some in the fridge.'

They had accepted him so easily—the rest of her family! The children treated him as casually as they treated Pete and Jim, and here was her mother suggesting an offer of a beer.

'You go and ask him, Mum,' she said. 'I'll finish the salads.'

'Hmm!'

'And what's that supposed to mean?' she demanded of her mother.

'What's what supposed to mean?' her infuriating relative replied.

'That "hmm" sound you made!' Marnie stormed. Then she heard the echo of her voice and grinned.

'Touchy, aren't I?' She gave her mother a quick hug. 'But you did go "hmm" and it did mean something. And you can just stop thinking it. Richard Cunningham's a neighbour and the kids like him and he'll be doing a few home visits with me, but that's it, Mum. There's no "hmm" to it at all.'

'If you say so, dear,' her mother said in such a placid, satisfied way that Marnie had to grit her teeth to prevent a further outburst of denials. 'But, in the meantime, if he's going to cook the dinner shouldn't we offer him a drink?'

CHAPTER NINE

'MARION is five months pregnant. She comes into town once a fortnight to see Dr Crail for a check-up, and attends my antenatal exercise classes.'

Marnie made this announcement as she was strapping herself into Richard's car next morning. Not that she'd expected anything other than a businesslike approach from him. After all, he'd been exemplary company the previous evening, right down to reading the twins their bedtime story and then inviting Kyle and Jill to walk up the drive with him when he headed home.

They could look at the stars, he'd said. He'd once studied astronomy but couldn't remember all he'd learnt. Maybe they knew some he didn't.

And they'd gone off all but wagging imaginary tails, so eager were they to spend more time with him!

'We go into town, then take the Weldon road,' she added as he steered the car back up her drive. 'On this visit we check that she has everything on the list—'

'The list?'

She glanced at him now and saw a suspicious puckering at the corner of his lips. Well, let him laugh! Businesslike she'd begun and businesslike she was going to stay.

'I give the families a list of what they'll need. Actually, it's three lists. What they'll need for the bed or birth place, what the woman will need for herself and what she'll need for the baby. On this visit I look at all the preparations. By now the couple have usually decided where they'll have the baby—'

'Where they'll have the baby?' he repeated, perplexed—not laughing now. 'Isn't the whole idea of a home birth that you have the baby at home?'

It was her turn to smile.

'Yes, but where at home is the next consideration. Perhaps you should wait and see. All I'll say is that bedrooms are fairly low on the list of favoured places. Kitchens are good because they usually have uncarpeted floors and are close to the supply of hot water. I check that it's a practical decision and make sure they've an alternative idea—in case, for instance, they want a water birth but the floor's not strong enough to hold a full tub of water.'

'Water birth? You do water births?'

He sounded so flabbergasted that she chuckled.

'Well, I've come close but never actually done one,' she admitted. 'But if you're still here in January you might be present at the first. Josie Williams, who lives in one of the houses up near Harriet's and Paul's, is expecting her second child. She was living near the coast when she had her first and the doctor there was enthusiastic and encouraging about the option. He'd even been to France to spend time with Dr Odent.'

'It's like a whole new field of medicine,' he murmured. 'A sub-culture I've heard practically nothing about in the city.'

'That could be because city doctors have much busier practices. Their appointment lists don't allow time for house calls, particularly not when it's something that can be as unpredictable and could take as long as a baby's birth.'

He nodded, then glanced towards her with a smile.

'And do you have a special list for water births?'

She fought the heart flutters caused by his smile and answered with assurance, pleased it was something she could recite without needing much brain power.

'Something to heat the water. If there's electricity involved I insist they have a qualified electrician check the wiring.'

She heard a faint repetition of her 'if' but decided he was better seeing things for himself, rather than listening to explanations.

'We use sea salt in the water to stop the skin going wrinkly so that's on the list, and as a woman often wants to get in and out of the bath—finding the different atmospheres a distraction—we need extra towels or cotton blankets to dry her and keep her warm.'

Richard felt his interest growing. At first he'd listened to her explanations to keep his mind off the distracting effect of her long, bare legs. Where else would the local midwife wear shorts to work? He was also distracted by a faint, flowery fragrance, which he assumed was perfume although it bore little resemblance to the sophisticated blends he had learnt to recognise.

Now he wanted to know more.

'I would have thought the women would be worried the baby might drown.'

She turned towards him with the first full-blown smile of the day—and he all but crashed into an oncoming vehicle! She's got four kids, he reminded himself. At the moment you're not certain you like kids!

'The midwife is far more worried about that than the parents,' she admitted. 'Most families who opt for water birth have read all the information they can find about it and other alternatives. They understand water is the natural environment for the foetus and that the baby's lungs are still folded when he or she is delivered. The cord continues to deliver oxygen until the baby takes its first breath, whether that's in an air birth or a water birth.'

'And the placenta? Does she deliver that in the water as well?'

He took his eyes off the road for long enough to see a tiny frown mar the smoothness of her forehead.

'I'm in two minds about that,' she told him. 'I'd prefer not, as I like to monitor the blood loss, but a lot of the literature suggests there's no problem.'

He found himself disturbed by her concern, as if he couldn't be at ease while she was worrying over something.

'Do you have professional support? Do you discuss all this with Dr Crail?'

She smiled again.

'I belong to the Midwives Association and to the Nursing Mothers Association, and to every other organisation or association that sends out literature about alternative methods of birth, but there's no one close by who does similar work, and Dr Crail—though supportive of home births—can't be bothered with too many "new-fangled" ideas!'

'He disapproves?'

She shook her head and her smile broadened.

'No, but he thinks I'm nuts to go along with them. "Tell them where you want them to have the baby, Marnie!",' she mimicked in a firm but 'old-man' voice. '"You're the one in charge!"'

He smiled at her portrayal, but was still disturbed by her lack of professional back-up.

'Would he come in an emergency?'

'Of course he would,' she assured him. 'And I always let the ambulance know when I go out for a delivery so they're aware they could be called if things go wrong. In many parts of England they have a flying squad for obstetric emergencies, but in a sparsely populated area like this we're flat out keeping a doctor.'

'So Marnie Wonderwoman does the lot.' He said it gently and glanced her way, knowing he'd see the colour creep into her cheeks.

'I don't do anything any other midwife wouldn't do!' she muttered, then directed his attention to the road. 'It's the next turn on the left. The sign says Bright Forest Road.'

Bright Forest Road. What a wonderful address for the expected baby! He saw the turn-off and slowed, then swung the car onto the unsurfaced track. Tall gums, stripped of bark at this time of the year and starkly white, lined the edges of the road. Richard marvelled at their beauty and felt a sense of peace and serenity sweep over him. Was the bush rejuvenating his soul, or was it this woman—his neighbour—who was bewitching him into such serendipity?

The house was a simple octagon, built from mud brick and river stone so that it looked, against the surrounding eucalypt scrub, like a new form of nature. The area close to the house had been cleared and planted with a riot of flowering plants and herbs. The blended perfume from the garden wafted into the car as they pulled up.

'It's a good bushfire precaution, growing non-native plants close to the house. In the rain-forest areas the risk is less, but in this timber country people must be aware of the dangers.'

She led the way through the garden, calling out to warn the residents that visitors had arrived.

'We're out the back—building the pool,' a voice replied, and a small child, clad only in a skimpy pair of shorts, appeared to lead them through a tangle of vines towards the back garden.

'It's like a scene from a picture-book,' Richard murmured as he took in the beauty of a garden where all the flowers were white. Petunias tumbled in wild array among rose bushes, jasmine and bell-shaped flowers he couldn't identify. In the centre of this magical scene stood a wooden pergola with a thick covering of pale-leafed grape vine.

All the activity in the yard was centred beneath the pergola. A large hole had been dug and three men, supervised by the small child and a pregnant woman, were smoothing the concrete sides with small trowels.

'I don't want it rough,' the woman said. 'I refuse to give the baby gravel rash on his first day in this world.'

'She'll have the baby here?' Richard muttered to Marnie, forgetting her admonition that he keep an open mind. 'What if it rains?'

'We'll rig a tarpaulin over the pergola,' the woman said, stepping lightly towards them.

She greeted Marnie with a warm hug while Richard struggled to come to terms with the idea.

'Isn't it a beautiful setting? We had the roses and jasmine here and then, as soon as I knew I was pregnant, I pulled out everything with coloured flowers and shoved them around the front, and planted white for purity.'

Marnie saved him from further embarrassment by performing a formal introduction.

'Marion's husband, Raoul, is the man in the red bandana at present in the pool. The other labourers are Ziggy and Jack—our local "go anywhere, tackle anything" building team, and the small foreman is Kye.'

Richard nodded to the men, recognising a new uneasiness within him as envy. For a mad moment he felt like stripping off his shirt and shoes and joining the men at work in the small pool.

How must it feel for Raoul—to be working with his hands on the birth-place for his baby?

'Are you going to stay outside and watch them work or come inside to see my routine?'

Marnie's voice left him in no doubt as to what he should do. After all, he'd talked her into letting him tag along with her. Yet he left reluctantly, aware that the special camaraderie he could sense between the men was something which was missing from his own life.

He must be lonely, he decided as he followed the two women into the house. He'd ring Jackie as soon as he got home and suggest she come for a few days. Perhaps ask Joe and Nancy to join them over the weekend. They could fly to Coolangatta and he'd drive across and collect them from there.

'I've got all the sterile things in this big paper bag,' Marion was explaining to Marnie as Richard entered the house. It was a huge, open space, separated into functions instead of rooms. At the far side a snowy white mosquito net hung from a brass chain, delineating a sleeping area. Nearby an alcove, made private by a brightly painted curtain, held a small mattress and wooden boxes filled with bright toys.

In the centre of the room was a circular stone fireplace with a copper hood above it. Chairs and beanbags were clustered cosily close, and more chairs stood around a table that looked like a small log split down the middle and opened up to form the flat top. The surface had been polished to a bright sheen, bringing to life the rich colour and beauty of the grain.

Marnie and Marion were bent over a wooden chest, and he could smell the camphor of its wood.

'It's so simple, yet so beautiful,' he murmured, and Marion straightened up and smiled at him.

'All we need or want or could wish for,' she told him. 'Such a relief after years of battling to have more and more "things".'

'But you have "things",' he said, pointing to a huge fuel stove, a gleaming copper kettle and a dresser with open shelves holding brightly painted pottery plates and mugs.

'Beautiful, practical things,' she pointed out. 'Nothing we don't need or use on a regular basis.'

He considered his city apartment, with its clustered glass tables, sleek leather armchairs and elaborate *en suite* with 'his' and 'hers' hand-basins. He'd been going out with an interior designer when he'd bought the place, and had let her have a free hand with the decoration.

It had quality art objects scattered casually on shelves and a state-of-the-art stereo system cleverly concealed in a marble pillar, but it had cost a fortune and lacked a soul, he realised now—lacked a sense of 'home'.

'Earth to Dr Cunningham! Are you reading us, Doctor?'

Marnie was frowning slightly, as if worried by his abstraction.

'Only just,' he admitted, smiling to banish her concern. 'It's got a feeling to it, this place. . .'

She nodded and returned his smile.

'Distilled happiness, I call it,' she said. 'I feel it in a number of the houses I visit.'

Her cheeks grew pink. Did she think he'd laugh at the fancy?

'Let's check your lists,' he said in a tight voice, while silently reminding himself of all the reasons why a romantic entanglement with this woman was impossible.

Marnie knew he was unsettled. She could feel the waves of his discomfort washing over her as he stood beside the chest and watched her count towels and sheets and cotton blankets.

'You're all set,' she told Marion. 'Well done!'

'I kept most of the things from when Kye was born,' she said. 'Now, how about we adjourn to the kitchen for a glass of lemonade, and your doctor friend can ask me anything he wants about water birth.'

My doctor friend?

Marnie glanced at him but he was still abstracted, looking around the room with the bemused air of a time-traveller.

She took his arm and steered him towards the kitchen area.

'Do you want to ask Marion any questions?' she whispered as Marion disappeared down into the stone-lined cellar to fetch the lemonade.

He looked towards her, then down at her hand which still held his forearm. She drew away.

'I think I'd better get my agent up and discuss the book with her,' he said in the same strained voice he'd used earlier.

'Before you start to write it?'

She watched him as she waited for his reply, puzzled by a mood that had swung from businesslike to introspective too suddenly. Then a smile tilted one corner of his mouth and he pulled himself together with an effort she imagined she could feel.

'Oh, I've already started it,' he said, 'but I'd better show her what I've done so she can sweet-talk the publishers into accepting it.' The smile disappeared and he was all control once again. 'Now, do you think Marion would mind if I taped our conversation?'

'Not in the slightest,' Marion answered, appearing up the cellar steps with a tall glass jug in her hand.

They settled at the table, sipping at the delicious drink while Marion recalled the details of Kye's birth.

'But why did you opt for water?' Richard asked.

Marion grinned at him.

'I love it!' she admitted. 'We were living over on the coast at the time. If I could afford to live on the edge of the ocean I would. Unfortunately, ocean-front land isn't available at dirt-cheap prices. The mountains are Raoul's spiritual home, but they're second best for me.'

'I can hardly use that as a scientific hypothesis for water birth,' Richard grumbled.

'Why not?' Marnie countered. 'The whole idea of home birth is about choice. You might ask fifty women why they choose water and get fifty different answers, but the important factor is their right to choose—within the limits of common sense and safety.'

'So no dawn-on-the-top-of-the-mountain births?' he teased.

'Not unless the parents-to-be provide me with a helicopter.'

She knew she was smiling witlessly at the man. Honestly, after all the admonitions she'd delivered to herself during the sleepless hours of the night, she was behaving like a. . .

What?

She heard Richard ask another question and Marion begin her reply, but she was too concerned with her own question.

A love-sick teenager?

What had Pete said? Don't be afraid of your feelings? Something like that! But she had to fear her feelings, to be wary of her attraction to this man who would be gone in another six weeks. And she had to protect not only herself but her precious family from the fall-out of his departure. Keep it casual—neighbourly!

'We could do the "earth to" routine again,' she heard Richard say and realised he'd been talking to her.

'Marion was telling me about your antenatal massage routines. Have you any literature on it?'

She nodded.

'Heaps of stuff. I'll bring it up to your place after dinner, if you like.' What a stupid suggestion! 'Or send Kyle up in the afternoon. That might be better—he could check on the state of your lawn,' she amended, almost choking on the words in her hurry to get them out.

'He did the lawn on Friday,' Richard pointed out—in a particularly neighbourly voice. 'If there's a lot of it I could pick it up when I drop you home.'

It made sense and she could hardly say, in front of Marion especially, that she didn't want him in her house more than was absolutely necessary. That she didn't want to see him looking so at home there! Particularly after last night when dreams of a completed 'family' had tormented her.

They inspected the pool again before they left, as well as the chip-heater Raoul had picked up at a second-hand store to heat the water.

'Remember you'll need protection from the wind as well as rain in case the weather's bad,' Marnie told the couple.

'We've a hip bath in the cellar,' Raoul told her. 'We'll bring it up and use it by the fire if it's that bad.'

'So all contingencies are covered?' Richard asked as they walked back through the garden towards the car.

Except a death, Marnie thought, remembering Saturday's sadness. She said nothing, not wanting to upset Marion, but Richard seemed to sense her mood for he moved closer and the slight brushing of their bodies gave her comfort.

Or had she imagined that? Had it been an accidental move on his part, pressing closer to avoid treading on the rambling garden plants?

She was still considering the questions when they reached her house. The conversation on the trip home had been purely medical and now his curt, 'I'll get the books some other time,' made her wonder what she'd done to upset him.

Not that it mattered, she told herself. It was much better this way.

Richard waited until she'd unlocked her front door, then drove off in an eruption of gravel and spinning of tyres.

He rubbed his arm, which still seemed to retain some imprint from her skin. He'd barely touched her yet the contact had fired something in his blood, and now his body ached with wanting her while his lips hungered for a kiss.

It was madness to think he could get involved with her. He was a writer—he needed peace and solitude, not four kids who seemed bent on self-destruction most times he met them. And it was ridiculous to even consider jeopardising Marnie Ferguson's happy family life to satisfy his own lustful urges. He liked her too much to do that.

Liked her too much? Liked the red-headed witch?

They argued every time they met! Where did liking come into it?

The argument took him up her drive and back down his own. He cut the engine and sat, listening to the silence. Maybe it was the silence, the isolation, getting to him. He'd phone Jackie and insist she come for a visit. After all, he was her prize author and he'd rarely demanded much of her time.

Jackie came the following afternoon, flying to Coolangatta then hiring a car and driving in from the coast with such promptness that he felt vaguely guilty.

'So, tell me about the new and wonderful idea,' she prompted when they were settled on the lower terrace, cool drinks in hand, watching the late afternoon shadows creep across the valley.

'It's on childbirth,' he said.

'That's obstetrics, not paediatrics,' she pointed out. 'Once you get out of your field you're sure to lose readers.'

'Maybe I will,' he said slowly, 'but I don't think that's important. I'd like it to be a reassuring kind of book— a "what to expect" book in the same way my other books tell parents what to expect as children grow and develop.'

He leaned forward, excited at finally putting his ideas into words.

'You know how I try to offer parents choices in how they handle situations, and always advise that children should also be offered alternatives? Well, why shouldn't that process be repeated in pregnancy? Women have choices in where and how they have their baby, about whether they want drugs or not, but this is fairly recent. Birth has had a medical model for perhaps the last five decades but it's turning back now to a more natural one these days. Yet how many of the standard "getting ready for baby" books include information on the options available and dispel myths about hospitals being the best option?'

Jackie smiled at him.

'Do I sense the conviction of a recent convert?' she teased, but before he could explain that he still knew very little a small voice distracted him.

'I'm sorry to bother you,' Mikey said politely, 'but you did say you'd take us into town to look at a tree one afternoon, and I just wondered which day because we'll have a lot to do, decorating it and the big one by the creek and getting everything ready for Christmas.'

He dropped a plastic bag beside Richard's chair.

'And Marnie sent these books.'

Richard felt obscurely pleased. The child could have used the books as an excuse for his visit and then asked his question, but he'd refused the ploy.

'I'm glad you reminded me,' he told Mikey. 'This is my friend, Jackie. She's just arrived today but I'm sure she'd like to visit Clareville with us tomorrow and help us find a tree. Would that suit you?'

He saw a gleam of delight in Mikey's dark eyes and the quick nod of the carrotty head. Mikey said a polite goodbye to Jackie and was about to walk away when he turned back towards Richard.

'And could you please phone Marnie and tell her it's all right and that we didn't badger you into taking us?' he asked.

'I'll tell her it was my suggestion,' Richard assured him, and watched the little figure scamper back towards the hole in the hedge.

'Your suggestion?' Jackie echoed. 'You suggested taking a child on an outing? I can remember a day not long before you went all rural when your sister asked you to mind her two for a few hours. You paid a clown to come and entertain them because you'd decided you'd written too much about kids to be able to talk naturally to them.'

He shifted in his chair, aware that his mind had been following Mikey through the hedge.

'It's not one child, it's either two or four we'll be taking,' he said, to divert the conversation away from his aberrant behaviour. 'The neighbour's kids. Her car's out of action at the moment. She's the local midwife, which is how I've got caught up in the birth-choices thing. Nice woman—you'll probably meet her one of these days.'

He was congratulating himself on sounding so off-hand about Marnie Ferguson when Jackie said, 'I see!' in a strained voice and began to talk about the Christmas appeal.

'But I've been so careful to preserve my anonymity,' Richard argued. 'I took my grandfather's name as a pseudonym so parents would still come to the "Richard Cunningham" me as a normal paediatrician, not some know-it-all expert.'

'But you're seeing fewer and fewer patients these days,' Jackie pointed out. 'You're lecturing more and writing more. It's valid work, Richard—'

'And it's taking me further and further from where I began. This childbirth experience has made me begin to re-think so many of my values and attitudes, Jackie. If doctors are unnecessary at a large percentage of births then you have to question the roles of specialists in so many other fields. Perhaps a competent GP can do more for the majority of children than a specialist who's another step removed from the family and the patients' environment.'

'I think that's an argument in favour of "coming out", not against it,' Jackie responded. 'And the Trust needs a high-profile figure to kick off the appeal. We've asked other well-known paediatricians and they've all shrieked excuses about Christmas being a family day.'

And I don't have a family! He glanced across towards the hedge. The twins fully expected him to spend Christmas with them, but no invitation had been forthcoming from Marnie.

And he didn't know that he wanted one.

Much!

Christmas in the city with Jackie and the false hoo-ha of a television station would be infinitely simpler—infinitely safer!

'You can go on TV as Gareth Gordon and not mention your real name, then only people who've actually met you or know you would realise who you are in your other life.'

'You've left out "and no one watches TV on Christmas Day anyway" from your arguments,' he told her, then he nodded. 'I suppose I could do it!'

As he heard the reluctance in his voice he realised that it wasn't because he'd lose his anonymity but because he was committing himself to something that would make it impossible to spend Christmas with Marnie and her brood.

If she asked him. . .

He was wondering if she would, planning his polite refusal, when she burst on to his desk.

'There is absolutely no necessity for you to drive the children to town to find a tree. I sent Mikey over here to give you the books you wanted, not to be asking favours—'

Something in the silence greeting her tirade warned Marnie she'd said enough. As Richard stood up she caught a glimpse of shapely legs in the chair beyond his—shapely legs clad in sheer stockings and neat black high-heeled shoes.

'I'm sorry, I didn't realise you had a visitor,' she said stiffly. 'Anyway, I only came to say I'd take the kids.' She had begun to back away but remembered something else she'd meant to tell him. 'Besides, it's not good for them to get their own way all the time. They have to learn that adults weren't put on earth to satisfy their every whim. You have to say no sometimes.'

'Not when I'd offered to take them,' he countered.

'Well, I don't know why you did that,' Marnie declared, 'considering you don't like kids very much.'

And, having delivered this parting shot, she turned and fled, aware that the rage which had prompted those final insulting words had been fired by shapely legs, not Richard.

He caught up with her as she bent to go through the hedge.

'I'll have you know I love kids!' he roared, seizing her shoulders and spinning her around to face him. 'And I'm taking them to town tomorrow. I don't make promises lightly. . .'

The tone of his voice faded from wrath to tenderness in the seconds it took to say the words, and his whispered, 'Oh, Marnie!' made her tremble.

His hands gentled and framed her face, then he bent and kissed her on the lips—one short and tender kiss of such sweetness that she felt like crying when it stopped.

'We've got to talk,' he sighed. 'I've my agent, Jackie, visiting for a few days—perhaps after that.'

His hands smoothed against her skin.

'Maybe it isn't so impossible. Maybe it isn't so ridiculous.'

She shrugged, then shook her head.

'Get home to your chickens, mother hen,' he said softly, and turned her towards the hedge.

She struggled through the tunnel, her mind churning his statements over and over again. Did he mean. . .? Was he saying. . .?

She made the other side, straightened up and dusted the twigs off her clothes.

How was she supposed to know what he meant? The sum total of her 'experience' was an innocent high-school romance with a boy who'd called her Red, and a few dates with a medical student when she was doing her nursing training—a relationship that had tended when he'd sulked after she'd told him she had no intention of having sex with him until she knew him better.

Pity she hadn't taken the same tack with Richard. Not that she *had* given in to the urging of her body, but she'd wanted to. Still wanted to, if she was honest.

Is that what he wanted to discuss? Would he say things like, 'We're attracted to each other; why not make the most of it'?

And could she handle such a question?

'Probably not!' she muttered, then added, 'Mother hen, indeed!'

And she headed into the house, determined to put the entire conversation out of her mind.

CHAPTER TEN

MARNIE was in town visiting Anne when Richard collected the children next day, and asleep—or pretending to be asleep—when he picked them up to go to the markets on the Sunday. And in between she'd managed to avoid him but not avoid thinking about him.

The twins had reported on Jackie, Margaret rabbiting on about her beautiful clothes and lovely red fingernails. The thought of the woman staying in the house with Richard made Marnie feel physically sick so she'd been 'out' the day they came again—on Wednesday—to string lights in the big tree down by the creek. In the flush of pre-Christmas goodwill all the kids were on 'Richard' and 'Jackie' terms by now, while even her mother had been singing the couple's praises and popping over for cups of tea.

Not that Marnie cared how perfect the neighbours were! But Richard shouldn't have said 'Oh, Marnie!' the way he had when he had another woman hanging around. It had unsettled her and made her think impossible things!

She'd collected her car on Friday then been called in to the hospital on Saturday night when a pregnant woman staying with friends in the town had gone into labour. In the end the delivery had been uncomplicated, but it had taken all night for the little boy to make his appearance and she'd come home—again—in the dawn light.

She heard the four of them calling goodbye to her mother, heard the deeper rumble of Richard's voice and

then drifted into an uneasy sleep, thick with dreams of
Richard—then suddenly alive with screams!

Dreadful screams, growing louder and louder.

In the house, not in her dream.

She flew out of bed to see Richard carrying Jill into
the house. The child was rigid in his arms and the
screams sliced through the air like glass through flesh.

'Take the twins through to the kitchen and talk to
them, Mum,' she said, reaching out to take Jill from
Richard's arms. The weight was too much for her so he
continued to support the child while Marnie soothed and
petted her, talking all the time.

'It's OK, love,' she murmured to the girl. 'It's OK,
you're safe now. I won't let anything happen to you.
See, Kyle's here, and Gran and the twins. We're your
family and we love you—we'll protect you.'

The screams subsided into whimpers, then Jill went
slack and her eyes rolled back in her head.

'Has she fainted? Is it a seizure of some kind? What
happened, Richard? What upset her like this?'

She dragged him towards Jill's bedroom and watched
as he rested the child gently on the bed. Marnie knelt
beside the bed and held the thin hand, still talking, soothing, reassuring, her eyes on Richard as he checked
Jill's pulse.

Jill moved, rolled onto her side, opened her eyes to
look at Marnie and then began to cry, her arms reaching
out for comfort.

Marnie shifted to the bed and cradled her, holding the
shaking body close to hers and talking, talking, talking—
hoping that words would take away whatever terror had
split the child's mind wide open.

Beside the bed Richard stood with Kyle, and Marnie
noticed they held each other's hands.

'Would you go out and tell the twins she's OK now?'
she asked Richard when the sobs had subsided into shud-
dering breaths and she felt the tension in the slight body
begin to ease.

He nodded, spoke to Kyle and left the room, returning
minutes later with both twins.

'They needed to see for themselves,' he said in an
undertone to her as Margaret came over to give Jill a
hug and Mikey stroked her arm.

Marnie could see the shadow of fear on their faces
and she brushed her hand reassuringly across the two
mops of red hair.

'I think Jill was frightened by something she
remembered,' she told them. 'So frightened she forgot
that she's safe now she's with us.'

'It was the Punch and Judy show,' Margaret confided
in a sibilant whisper. 'When one of the puppets hit the
other puppet again and again—'

'We'll tell Marnie about it later,' Richard declared,
and he scooped Margaret into his arms and nudged
Mikey in front of him towards the door. 'Right now Jill
needs to sleep. Sleep is the best thing for people who've
had a shock.'

As they left the room Mikey asked the inevit-
able 'why', and Marnie decided that her two youngest
were handling their own shock quite well—with
Richard's help!

And Jill *was* sleeping, naturally this time, her breathing light and even and her cheeks regaining a little
colour. Marnie settled her on the bed, then sat beside
her, stroking back the long silky hair.

'Margaret's right,' Kyle said quietly. 'I'd been trying
to remember when she started screaming and it was
when Judy was hitting Punch with a stick. Not at first,

but after the hitting had gone on for a while. Richard
had a mobile phone and I rang Dr Crail while he drove,
but Dr Crail was out on a call so we brought her
straight home.'

He hesitated, his eyes downcast and one foot kicking
at the heel of the other, then he raised his head and
looked Marnie in the eyes.

'Will she be all right?' he asked, and she heard a
tremor of despair in the words.

'I think she might be better than all right,' Marnie
assured him. 'I'm not a psychologist but you know we've
always thought something terrible must have happened
to her—something so bad she had to run away. Perhaps
she stopped speaking because she didn't want to think
about it or talk about it. Maybe she saw someone hit a
person she loved and the show reminded her. It gave
her a fright, but it might help her get better now she's
faced that awful memory.'

Kyle nodded.

'I doubt a psychologist could have put it better.'

She glanced up and saw Richard in the doorway.

'Your gran's pouring drinks and serving biscuits in
the kitchen. Do you want me to stay here with Jill and
Marnie while you stockpile a bit of food?'

Kyle shook his head.

'I won't leave her,' he said. 'I promised her that at
the coach terminal so I can't go back on my word.'

'I thought you'd say that so I brought you a tray.'

Marnie watched her mother bustle into the room, a
well-stocked tray balanced between her good hand and
her plastered arm. 'I'll sit here with Jill and Kyle for a
while,' she said to Marnie. 'You take Richard into the
kitchen and get him a cup of coffee. You have a break

now because you'll want to sit up with her tonight in case she wakes and I'm no use to you at night.'

She paused for breath, then smiled at Richard.

'I nod off in the chair within minutes of getting comfortable. How Marnie works the hours she does, I can't imagine. It'd be no good for me.'

Richard took the tray from her and gave it to Kyle, who'd settled himself on the end of Jill's bed. Then he pulled the chair from the desk and set it beside the bed.

'You'll be more comfortable with something behind your back, Betty,' he said, then he reached out and took Marnie's hand, helping her up from her position on the bed.

'Come on,' he bullied her. 'You heard your mother! You're to make me a cup of coffee.'

She went with him, enjoying the feel of her hand in his but deeply concerned about the little girl she considered her daughter. The twins were playing in 'their' corner of the living room, debating every stage of whatever game it was—but quietly, for a change.

Richard led her to the kitchen.

'Actually, the coffee's made,' he told her with a smile that made her knees sag. 'I wanted to talk to you and your mother thought you'd probably need a carbohydrate boost to cope with your own shock.'

'Was Margaret right?' she asked as he poured coffee into two mugs and added sugar to one of them. 'Was it Judy hitting Punch that affected her?'

She saw him frown and guessed he was trying to replay the scene in his mind.

'They'd finished bu- looking around the stalls and we were about to leave when we heard the music from a tent on the far side of the field. Actually, it was coming from behind the tent and as soon as I saw the set-up I knew it was a Punch and Judy show. I'd seen one once in England at an old-time fair but I didn't think they were about much these days.'

'I've heard of them but never seen one,' Marnie agreed, sipping at her coffee.

'They were probably banished by the thought police!' Richard suggested. 'Although they were supposedly fun things for kids they were very violent. In the usual story-line Judy bashes Punch to death, then the policeman comes to take her away. In the past, I suppose the kids who watched the shows knew Punch would reappear later. They'd scream for him and he'd appear around the corner of the curtain where Judy and the policeman couldn't see him.'

'A mischief-maker, but not a horror story?' Marnie asked, trying to imagine the scene.

'Apart from the bashing,' Richard said, his voice strained and sober.

'So we guess she saw. . . What, Richard? A woman hitting a man? Does that seem likely? Or was it the motion of hitting and hitting and hitting? Kyle told me it went on and on. Could someone have hit her mother, perhaps? Would she transfer the motion of a woman hitting a man to a man hitting a woman?'

'Whoa!' he said, holding up both hands in a surrender signal. 'One question at a time.'

He smiled again and waved towards the verandah.

'Want to sit outside and talk about it?' he asked.

She nodded, dismayed to find her body reacting to his presence when all her concentration should be on Jill.

'Gran and Kyle are in with Jill, and Richard and I will be sitting on the deck,' she called to the twins.

She was surprised to hear Richard add, 'We need to talk for a while—is that OK?'

Two voices chorused their understanding and Marnie followed him out onto the deck. At times he was nearly as good with the kids as Gareth Gordon would be. She settled into a chair, accepted a bun from a plate he offered towards her and said, 'Well?'

'To begin, the show was in an old-style tent and the puppets' clothes were old-fashioned. Punch wore a lovely satin coat and to a child who hadn't seen the show before could easily have been a woman.' He paused for a moment and Marnie wondered what he was thinking.

'At first I'd assumed all the kids were yours,' he said slowly. 'Then you told me about the twins, and other things have made me realise that Kyle and Jill have come into your life relatively recently. How, Marnie? And why? Do you foster children? Disturbed children? What history do you have for Jill? I know you hoped time and love would cure her, but now that this has happened we need to know more.'

'We don't know much,' she said, 'and it starts with Kyle.'

Richard nodded.

'He said something in the car—something about finding her.'

It was Marnie's turn to nod.

'Do you know the Gold Coast?' she asked.

'Holiday haven? I know it, although I prefer my holidays in quieter, less glittery places.'

'It has its quiet spots but I'll argue that with you some other time,' Marnie told him. 'Anyway, my mother, who's a whizz-bang bridge player, has a home there. It was our holiday house when we were kids and she went to live there after Dad died.'

She sighed and listened to a pair of butcher birds complaining to each other.

'When Katherine was diagnosed she wanted peace and quiet so we came here. Mum stayed on with me after Katherine died until the twins started pre-school, then she began to divide her time between here and the house on the coast.'

'No doubt urged on by you doing your independent act!' Richard murmured, and Marnie felt her cheeks grow hot.

'She's entitled to her own life!' she muttered. 'Anyway, one evening she was coming out of the bridge club on the highway and this kid came up and snatched at her handbag. She clouted him with her umbrella and by the time he'd recovered from the shock of an old lady fighting back she had a firm grip on his arm.'

Richard was smiling as if he could picture the scene.

'Kyle?'

'Kyle!' she affirmed. 'Mum told him she wasn't going to give him any money but he could come home with her and have a decent meal. Knowing Mum, I doubt whether she gave him time to argue but dragged him along with her, anyway.'

'I've heard runaways and street kids seem to gravitate to the Gold Coast,' Richard said, frowning now. 'Was he one of them?'

Marnie nodded again.

'It took a while to get the full story but it seems his mother died of a drug overdose and the de facto step-father took to beating Kyle. So he packed up what clothes he had, stole money from the fellow and headed north. He was lucky because there are good support services for these kids in Surfers' Paradise, which is the tourist centre of the Gold Coast. There's a place where they can get a midday meal and a sandwich to take with them for tea. He settled into his own new lifestyle, sleeping out in summer and in refuges in winter.'

She paused, considering the uncertainty of such an existence, then continued, 'He'd seen his mother's dependence on drugs and hated any form of substance abuse so that kept him safe from some of the more extreme behaviour of his new peers.'

Richard shook his head.

'We're failing all our children if we fail these kids,' he said sadly. 'What's wrong that we can't provide a safe environment for every child? That kids like Kyle are reduced to bag-grabbing?'

'I don't know any answers—only facts,' she told him. 'I've actually had words with Kyle's grandparents— sterling, upright folk who threw his mother out when she was fifteen, addicted and pregnant. That baby died and she cleaned up her act then when Kyle was born she contacted her parents again. They refused to believe she'd changed and that was that.'

She saw the shock on Richard's face and added softly, 'I can't blame them entirely. How do you cope with a tearaway daughter? I haven't had to face that yet.'

'I suppose blame is counter-productive,' Richard agreed, 'but that doesn't stop me wanting to hit someone! And we haven't come to Jill! Go on!'

'Mum and Kyle talked and Mum offered him a bed, but he was as wary as a stray cat—told her his mates were expecting him at the shelter. Come any time you need something, Mum told him. I won't make you stay, or keep you here against your will, but one day you might need a place to sleep for a while. Then she gave him a lecture on bag-snatching as a way of life and pointed out that he could get a homeless allowance from the government or an even better allowance if he went back to school.'

'I didn't know that,' Richard interrupted, and Marnie smiled.

'A number of the high schools on the Gold Coast actually organise shared accommodation for these kids and help them fill out all the forms. They teach them to budget their allowance—'

'And your mother knew all this?'

'She'd been a school counsellor for many years,' Marnie explained. 'Psychology degree and all!'

She smiled at his surprise.

'And I was telling you the child needed counselling when you had help on hand all along!'

Marnie bent forward and set her mug on the floor. Why was it so easy to talk to Richard about all of this? She doubted she'd told Pete as much.

'Mum prefers her "Gran" role, and tries to stick to that,' she admitted. 'But she did advise time and love with Jill.'

'With Jill? We're still on Kyle.'

'Kyle found Jill at the bus stop. Can we turn on the television?' Mikey offered the information to Richard, then turned towards Marnie with his question.

'May we,' she corrected automatically. 'Yes!'

She watched him run back into the house.

'That's it in a nutshell,' she admitted. 'Mum didn't see Kyle again until late one night. Kyle, who'd had words with someone at the shelter, had decided to spend the night in the coach terminal in Surfers' Paradise. At about three in the morning a coach pulled in and, among a host of passengers, a family got out. When everyone was gone he noticed Jill. She'd been near the family earlier, but remained behind when they left. After a while he spoke to her, asked her where she was going. She said, "I ran away" and "I'm Jill" and didn't speak again.'

'Weren't there adults about—people selling tickets, checking luggage, that kind of thing?'

'There were, but when Kyle pointed out that the child was on her own the man in charge said he'd have to call the police and Jill started screaming. In the end, Kyle took her hand and ran with her, hoping she'd stop the noise when she ran out of breath. He knew she was far too young to share his lifestyle—that she'd never survive on the streets. Poor kid, he had no idea what to do—'

'Until he remembered your mother!'

'Exactly,' she told him.

'But the child must have had family somewhere,' Richard objected. 'What about missing person reports? The police? Formalities?'

Marnie smiled as she remembered her mother's ferocious defence of Jill's right to privacy and Kyle's refusal to let anyone take Jill away.

'My mother contacted the police, who'd had no notice of a missing child matching her description. That was strange in itself.'

Richard got up and paced the deck as if he needed movement to help him listen.

'Usually, if a young girl goes missing, it's plastered across every newspaper and television station in the country,' he commented.

'And this wasn't!' Marnie said flatly. 'Predictably enough, the police brought in welfare people, but Jill screamed and shrank away, clinging to Kyle with such strength that his skin showed bruises later. My mother pointed out that they'd get nothing from her in this state. She took photographs herself, when Jill was with Kyle on the beach and looked relaxed and happy, and gave some to the police, then she announced that the child needed time to get over whatever had happened and she was taking her to the country.'

'And they let her?' He sounded so disbelieving that she straightened in her chair. 'I've worked with Children's Services—they have more rules and guidelines and red tape than the tax department.'

Marnie smiled.

'They also had my mother registered as a foster parent. She'd taken in young offenders for years. Pete and Katherine and I grew up never knowing who'd be sharing our bedrooms for a week or a month—or a few years, in some cases. Jim, who sometimes minds the kids when I'm called out, was one of our "brothers". It was because we'd visited him here and come to know and love the valley that Katherine decided this is where she wanted to live.'

His pacing brought him back towards her chair where he stopped. His hand brushed across her hair, then his fingers lingered on her neck.

'And that's that?'

'Not quite.' She managed to produce the words, but her skin tingled from the touch and her weak flesh trembled beneath it. 'Mum's been searching for some clue to Jill's identity ever since. When she wasn't reported missing we had to assume that her prime carer, whether mother, father or grandparent, had died. Mum has a friend in the police force and he searches through files in his spare time. If he comes up with a lead that looks likely Mum follows it up.'

'You're an enterprising lot,' he murmured, as his restless hand lifted the hair from her nape and let it fall back through his fingers. 'Where have you been looking?'

'Down south, for the most part. Mum checked the coaches that had come in that night. There were a few from Brisbane but the two long-distance arrivals were from the south. The police contacted the drivers, eventually, but although all could remember families travelling with them none of them remembered a family which seemed to have acquired a spare child along the route.'

'So what now?' Richard asked, dragging himself forcibly away from Marnie and the magic of her lustrous hair.

He saw her shudder and wished he'd stayed closer. The urge to protect her—to protect all this family—was growing stronger and stronger.

'I suppose we have to look at murder victims,' she said slowly. 'Go back to the police and see if they can connect up the date of her arrival on the Gold Coast with a severe bashing or murder anywhere.'

He saw her swallow as she spoke and knew the full horror of Jill's experience was suddenly hitting her. He was by her chair again in two swift strides.

'Hey!' he said gently, kneeling down so he could put an arm around her shoulders and hold her. 'It must have been a horrific shock for Jill at the time, but she's had what—about twelve months—of loving care since it happened. She's secure in this family and in the little world in which she moves. Having that shock today might be a good thing. She might be ready now to talk about what happened.'

He turned so he could look into her eyes.

'It will help her heal—to talk about it,' he reminded her. 'Telling someone will help to ease the load she's been carrying. You wouldn't want her carting such horrific baggage around with her for ever.'

She nodded slowly, then bent her head so that it rested

against his chest. He touched his lips to her hair and felt the rigidity leave her body.

'Why are you cuddling Marnie?'

Mikey's voice held polite interest—nothing more—but it was enough to make her pull away from him, breaking the contact. She straightened in her chair and smoothed her hair, while colour fluctuated deliciously in her cheeks.

'She was sad about Jill,' he explained as Margaret arrived to join in the conversation.

'I'm sad about Jill, too,' she piped up, looking hopefully at him. His heart jolted unexpectedly and he held out his arms, then hugged the little body that hurtled into them.

He looked up to see Marnie watching him, her eyes dark with questions she wouldn't ask and he couldn't answer.

'I'll put something on for dinner,' she muttered, standing up and looking out across the valley. 'Will you stay?'

He tried to read the inflection of the words but could find nothing to give him any clue as to whether she wanted him here or was being polite.

'Please stay,' Margaret whispered, her breath hot against his neck.

'I'd like that,' he said to Marnie, and thought he saw a shadow of a smile as she turned towards the kitchen.

Kyle was asleep in the spare bed and Richard, who'd insisted on sharing the dark vigil, had gone to make more coffee when Jill began to stir uneasily, coming out of the blessed oblivion of sleep to a frightening reality.

Marnie stroked the hair back from her face and murmured soothing sounds of love, but the nightmare had returned and Jill shook and whimpered even when

Marnie shifted to the bed and held the the girl tightly in her arms.

'Should we try a sedative?' she whispered to Richard when he returned.

He frowned and shook his head.

'Try talking—asking questions,' he suggested, setting the two coffee-mugs on Jill's desk and coming to sit beside the bed where he could touch them both.

Marnie hesitated, but Richard's hand pressed against her shoulder and gave her the courage she needed.

'Will you tell me about it, darling?' she asked the shaking child. 'Tell me what happened to frighten you like this. We love you so much, Jilly, but we can't help you if we don't know. I'm here, and Kyle's here, and Richard's here. We all want to help.'

The tremors eased slightly, and Jill moved so that her face was pressed hard against Marnie's chest. And when the words came they were muffled and hesitant—and so heart-rending that Marnie could feel the tears sliding unchecked down her cheeks.

'I used to sleep in Mum's bed sometimes. One night she woke up and pushed me under the bed,' the whispering, scratchy voice began. 'She told me to keep quiet and not come out whatever happened, but she cried and cried and I heard him hitting her. Over and over, the noise like the show today. Then I must have gone to sleep—'

Marnie heard the self-condemnation in Jill's voice and began to understand the true enormity of her daughter's burden.

'Darling one, you couldn't have helped. You couldn't have saved her if you'd come out. All that would have happened is that you'd have been beaten up yourself.'

Her tears coursed faster, choking the words as she rocked Jill to and fro.

'You mustn't feel guilty, Jilly. There was nothing you could do.'

'There was blood, Marnie, so much blood. And she wouldn't talk to me.'

The frail body shuddered at the memory and Marnie held her tighter.

'I ran away!' the child cried, remorse and pain piercing the air with their agony. 'The man hit my mother and first I hid and then I ran away.'

'Even grown-up people run away from things that hurt them,' Richard said, moving so that he, too, could hold the child. 'We run away from things we don't understand as well. And one of the things that's hardest to understand is why people hurt other people, Jill. That's a tricky question for grown-ups as well as children. All we can do is try to be different ourselves.'

Marnie felt the strength of his arm around her back, then Jill moved, her head inching away from its resting place until she could look up into Richard's face.

'I covered her with a blanket,' she whispered, totally destroying the last remnants of Marnie's composure. 'That was right, wasn't it?'

Richard nodded and smiled, then he reached out and touched Jill's cheek.

'It was the best thing you could have done,' he assured her. 'Now, would you like something to eat before you go back to sleep?'

He's telling me to act normally, Marnie realised, biting back an urge to throw herself onto the bed and sob her heart out.

'I'd like a glass of milk, please,' Jill told him, then

she turned to Marnie and whispered, 'And I'd better go to the bathroom!'

Marnie smiled through her tears and helped her off the bed. Jill's hand found hers and clung there so, while Richard got the milk, she stayed beside her child, trying to act 'normally'—whatever that might be—while horrific images battered at her brain.

'She's sleeping again,' Richard pointed out an hour later. 'I'm going to get you a hot drink of some kind, then pack you off to bed. I'll stay with her till morning.'

'I couldn't sleep, Richard,' she said, her quiet words bleak with pain. 'Every time I blink I picture that gruesome scene. How has she managed to live with that memory?'

'She's managed to live because you've provided her with all that love and security you once talked about,' he told her, drawing her to her feet and enfolding her in his arms. 'She's even started to put it behind her because you've given her such unconditional acceptance in your family, in your life and in your heart.'

He pressed her close and his lips moved against her hair, but she must have imagined him saying, 'Would that I had as much!'

Mustn't she?

CHAPTER ELEVEN

RICHARD sent her to bed and stayed with Jill so his presence next morning at breakfast seemed quite normal.

Then Jill said, 'Don't be so bossy, Margaret!' and the twins threw their arms around her and hugged her until she nearly choked.

'Keep talking to us,' Mikey whispered, as Marnie drew him away and tried to settle him down at the table once again.

She hadn't had time to talk to Richard about how they should behave towards Jill now—whether they should make a fuss or just go on as if nothing had happened.

'Let the kids do whatever comes naturally to them,' he said quietly after she'd sent the children outside to play and was clearing the table. 'There's no school for six weeks so they've time to adjust to a "talking" sister.'

She turned towards him and smiled weakly. She was embarrassed and grateful and full of something that felt like love but might be lust—and which he probably didn't want if it was love, anyway! Talk about confused!

'Thank you!' she mumbled, trying to gather enough wandering brain cells to make coherent conversation. 'For staying last night and being so understanding and helpful. And letting me sleep. You must be exhausted yourself.'

He reached out and grasped her shoulders.

'I don't want your gratitude, Marnie Ferguson,' he said gruffly. 'And, while I might not be exhausted, I'm too tired to string the words together to say the things I want to say. I'll go home and sleep, and call down later.'

He bent his head and kissed her gently on the lips.

But somehow later never came. Not the 'later' she'd been hoping for. He joined their lunchtime picnic by the creek, swimming with the children, sitting talking to Gran on the bank, cuddling Margaret, teasing Mikey and discussing soccer tactics with Kyle.

And he stayed for dinner, lighting the barbeque, cooking steak and sausages—providing seductive images of a completed family—and stirring Marnie's pulses every time he spoke, or laughed, or moved towards her.

Then, after dinner, when the short grey twilight had crashed to the darkness of the swift summer night he turned to the children.

'Well, kids, we adults have been doing all the work. Now it's your turn. How about you entertain us?'

Mikey looked at Kyle, then turned to him.

'A concert?' he said. 'You mean, have a concert?'

'Why not?' Richard replied, and something in his voice made Marnie look more closely at him.

Kyle ushered the excited children off the verandah, then came back to say they'd be ten minutes and would they please shift their chairs down to the far end? Richard stood up and began to drag the table back against the wall.

'What's going on?' Marnie demanded, moving her chair obediently back to make room for a 'stage'. 'Mum?'

Her mother shook her head.

'No one ever tells me anything!' she complained. 'So why would I know more than you?'

'Wait and see,' Richard said, putting his chair beside hers and sitting down so close she fancied she could hear him breathing.

Above them the stars appeared, bright fairy lights in the deep purple sky. Then someone turned out the light so that the watchers were in darkness while the 'stage' area was lit by the soft glow of the Christmas lights Richard and Kyle had rigged along the verandah rail.

Music blared, Kyle counted and the four children appeared, whirling and dancing with such precision that Marnie was stunned.

'They've had to practise this!' she muttered at Richard.

'Remember the barn!' he said, taking her hand in a casual clasp.

She watched in silence, unable to believe the professionalism of the children's performance. True, the moves were simple—kicks and twirls mainly—but they kept the beat and moved in time, Mikey's lips moving as he counted!

'Watch Jill,' Richard whispered, and she felt a swift stab of disappointment. He'd seen it before! He knew things about her children they'd kept secret from her. Then her eyes were drawn to Jill and she saw the fluid beauty of the girl's movements.

'Is there a ballet teacher in town?' he asked quietly, and she turned towards him.

'It would help? Give her something special to think about, to concentrate on?'

She was so excited by the idea she could barely get the words out.

'I'd thought of art lessons, but ballet? Do you think it might be the answer?'

He squeezed her fingers and, still watching the dying moments of the performance, murmured, 'You had the answer all along, you foolish woman! It was love and time and security. But ballet might be something extra—

might give her an opportunity to express herself in another way.'

'So she could dance away the pain,' Marnie murmured. She shook her head. 'I'd never have thought of it.'

The dancing ended and Marnie leapt to her feet, hugging each of the children and praising their efforts.

'You were all wonderful,' she said. 'Really fantastic! I know how much you must have practised to get it right.'

'Kyle made the steps easy so we could all do them, but Jill's the best,' Margaret told her.

'I noticed that,' Marnie replied, and reached out to give Jill a special hug. Out of the corner of her eye she saw Richard herding the others into the house and knew he'd left her with Jill deliberately. She drew Jill onto her knee and cuddled her.

'Did you learn ballet before?' she asked, and was surprised when the child shook her head.

'But my mother danced,' Jill told her, pressing her face into the curve of Marnie's neck.

'Then so should you,' Marnie told her firmly. 'Would you like to have ballet lessons?'

She felt the nod and tightened her arms around Jill's body.

'I'll arrange for you to start after Christmas,' she promised. 'Do you want to talk some more about your mother?'

'She was pretty and had yellow hair and worked at night—dancing, I think,' Jill whispered. 'The lady in the flat next door looked after me till Mum came home. Her name was Janet and she was old, like Gran, but I didn't have a gran—not one I knew.'

'We'll find out about your mother,' Marnie promised. 'You know our gran's been looking all year without any luck, but now we know about Janet that will help.'

So would the name of a town, she thought, but she was reluctant to force Jill's memory.

'You two want some supper?' Gran called, and Jill eased herself from Marnie's lap.

'We're coming,' she answered, then she turned to Marnie and smiled with real delight at hearing her own voice.

'You'll do, kid!' Marnie said to her, hiding her own rush of emotion behind a playful shove in the direction of the kitchen.

Richard raised his eyebrows as they came in and she nodded, then realised how easy such silent communication was with this man. Easy—and special—and dangerously seductive.

He'd become part of their lives, she realised two days later. Her mother had gone over to the Gold Coast to chase up the new leads on Jill's background, turning her attention now to more stark possibilities. And Richard had filled in as chauffeur, child-minder and chief organiser of the Christmas shopping.

He'd been friendly, neighbourly, wonderful with the children—but had never sought her out or spoken of what he'd intended saying the afternoon he'd said, 'Oh, Marnie!'

At times she wondered if she'd imagined that strange, abrupt conversation, then she'd notice a certain warmth in his smile, or a glint of something in his eyes that stirred her blood, and she guessed that the uncertainty she'd glimpsed once before lurked beneath his cheerful, neighbourly front. It was as if he was waiting for something, and filling in the time by proving what a wonderful family man he could be when he tried.

But why was he trying? It puzzled her but the weather had turned sultry and she found it impossible to think about simple things—let alone consider the convoluted workings of Richard Cunningham's mind.

'You can't possibly need all this food for Christmas dinner,' he complained as he helped her load the Christmas shopping into the back of his car. 'Hot Christmas dinners are a hangover of colonial times, yet here's a modern woman buying a turkey that will take four hours to cook on a sweltering hot summer's day!'

'We've always had turkey and cranberry sauce and ham and baked vegetables and steamed pudding—even when we were kids and spent Christmas at the beach,' Marnie told him, lifting the last of the bags into the car. 'Our one concession to summer is icy cold watermelon afterwards!'

'But you've enough food to feed a medium-sized army!' he grumbled, as he caught a watermelon which was trying to escape.

'Well, Mum will be back—you know she's gone up north to see the police about a man who murdered a woman and child at the time Jill disappeared. It seems he admitted killing the woman but consistently denied knowing anything about the child and, as her body was never discovered, we're assuming he might be telling the truth and that the child could be Jill.'

He nodded, and said gravely, 'Even if you don't tell her now, eventually she will want the details filled in.'

Marnie watched him push the watermelon back into place, seeing his hands move. . .

'But your mother being back hardly justifies two ton of foodstuffs.' He diverted the conversation—and her wandering attention—back to her shopping.

'And Pete will be here, and Jim and his wife and two

kids are coming,' she added hastily, then hesitated. Her four had been at her all week to ask Richard, but she knew how disappointed she would be if he said no and she was afraid to put it to the test.

She wiped away the sweat that was trickling into her eyes, drew a deep breath and turned to face him.

'Will you join us?' she asked, her heart thumping in her chest. She tried to sound casually unconcerned—as if his answer wasn't of any particular importance. 'After all, you've bought the tree, decorated the house and garden, entertained the kids and done most of the shopping. It's as much your Christmas as it is ours.'

He looked down into her eyes, read the uncertainty in them and felt an uncontrollable urge to take her in his arms and kiss it away. He wanted to tell her he loved her and that he'd spend every Christmas with her for the rest of his life, but caution made him hold his tongue.

I'm afraid I have to go to Sydney on Friday,' he said, trying to ignore the disappointment that shadowed her face. 'I'll stay down for Christmas Day and will probably fly back early next week.'

'The children will be disappointed,' she muttered, and sent the shopping trolley flying across the car park with an almighty push.

He watched her chase after it, kicking himself for unnecessary brutality, but he knew he must move slowly in this situation. It wasn't only his future and Marnie's at stake but the future of the four children. He couldn't come into their lives as something more than a friend, then walk away if the attraction between himself and Marnie didn't work out.

As each day passed, however, he realised how much he wanted it to work out—hoped and prayed that it would.

So why wasn't he putting it to the test?

He asked himself the question as she strode back towards him, her burst of temper dissipated by the chase after the trolley. She was practical and competent, a sensible loving mother—carrying, without any reluctance or regret, burdens no ordinary person would take on. Yet he guessed at a vulnerability beneath that calm exterior and an innocence he could destroy if he betrayed her in any way.

And it was the innocence that bothered him in other ways. He knew she was attracted to him, but he wondered if it was the attraction of love or simply a physical thing. Her social life must have been gravely restricted by having two, then four children.

'Well, are you going to stand there staring into space all afternoon or are you going to drive me home?' she asked crossly.

He looked down and saw beads of perspiration around her hair-line and a pinkness in her cheeks which hadn't come from chasing shopping trolleys.

He lifted his hand and wiped the droplets away.

'I wouldn't want to hurt you for the world,' he said quietly. 'It's put me into the very devil of a situation.'

He shook his head and sighed, then walked around the car to open the passenger door for her.

'I suppose the whole gang will be at home when we get back?'

She nodded, then shot him a fulminating look.

'And you don't have to entertain them,' she told him as she climbed into the high seat. 'They're perfectly capable of doing most things for themselves. You have your book to write, remember, and I suppose you have to pack.'

He chuckled at the bitchy comment and reached out to rest one hand against her cheek.

'I was beginning to think you were too good to be true,' he said softly, then he forgot all his mental caution and leaned forward to kiss her on the lips.

It was a good thing he was going away, he decided as they drove home in silence. He glanced towards her but her profile told him nothing, Was she as shocked by that kiss as he had been? He'd meant it as a teasing salute, but bells had clanged and drums had rolled and his heart had cavorted through at least a dozen dance steps.

Being away from her would give him time to think it through and decide—

Decide what? Whether to love her and leave her, or settle for a bit of the domesticated bliss he'd spurned up until now? The first was no option while the second was full of 'buts' that had no apparent resolution—not the least of which was geographical.

'Thank you for all your help,' she said as he dropped the last of the plastic bags of shopping on the kitchen bench. 'If I don't see you before Friday, then have a great Christmas.'

She sounded as cold and bleak as the snow on the Christmas cards that hung around the walls.

'I'll come down tomorrow,' he assured her. 'I've some small gifts for the children.' He wanted—needed—to say more, but couldn't find the words. He looked down towards the creek. He could hear the shouts and chatter of the children and knew they were working on a small dam and waterfall at the top end of the swimming hole.

'I've got to go to Sydney,' he said lamely. 'There's something I have to do, and so much to tell you, explain to you. . . Damn it, woman, don't look at me like that. I'm trying to work out what's best for all of us, for you and the kids as well as me, don't you see? It's not enough that I love you, Marnie Ferguson. There are four children's futures at stake here. Oh, I love them, too—don't think I don't. If I didn't care about them it would be easy.'

Marnie heard the words buried in his tirade and smiled, obviously annoying him even more.

'And don't smile at me like that!' he growled. 'You make it worse, and harder, and more complicated.'

Then he kissed her, a rough, passionate kiss that rekindled the flames he'd started earlier and stole her breath.

'And there's something I should have told you right at the beginning, and now I don't know how to do that either!' he growled as he thrust her away and stormed from the room. 'I've totally lost my senses!'

His final words floated back to her, but she didn't mind the implications. She'd totally lost hers as well.

She was out when he came on Thursday, taking her antenatal class in town. The children had given him the gifts they'd made for him and he'd promised he'd keep them until Christmas morning.

'He sent his love to you,' Margaret told her later. ' "Give Marnie my love and tell her I'll phone her," he said, then he went off to catch a plane.'

She felt bereft, unable to hide her disappointment.

'He told me he wasn't going until Friday,' she muttered.

'Change of plan,' Kyle said cheerfully. 'Something about seeing if he could tape his bit on Friday instead of doing it live. Sounds like television, doesn't it?'

She frowned at him.

'Richard? On television? Why would he be doing that?'

Kyle shrugged.

'He's a doctor, isn't he? Maybe he's famous and he's going to go on that children's appeal they have on Christmas Day. You know the one—you can ring up and give money.'

Marnie nodded, feeling more depressed every moment.

It had been hard enough to imagine any man in his right mind being interested in a woman with four kids— particularly a man as good-looking as Richard. But if he was famous it quadrupled the improbability! Famous men were usually also rich—and rich and famous men had their pick of women! Even she knew that.

Yet he'd said he loved her. . .

And said that love wasn't enough, her stout common sense reminded her.

'So, can we watch that show on Christmas Day?' Kyle was asking.

She nodded, breaking her own rule that television was not turned on during daylight hours.

He came on at nine. Pete was still in bed, having arrived late the night before, but she, her mother and the children were all sitting on the floor in the living room in a drift of wrapping paper and presents. The exquisite crystal bird the children had given her was set on a table by the window, refracting the bright summer light into tiny rainbows.

'There's Richard,' Margaret shouted. 'There he is!'

And Marnie looked across in time to hear the end of the introduction.

'Noted paediatrician and author, Dr Gareth Gordon.'

'Dr Gareth Gordon!' the children chorused, turning from the set to stare at Marnie.

'Maybe he's got a twin,' Gran suggested, but Marnie knew it was Richard.

She dropped her head into her hands, groaning as she remembered quoting his words at him.

'I hoped I'd get here first,' a deep voice said, and she looked up and frowned at the television screen.

'It's Richard, it's Richard!' the children were shouting as they made a concerted dash for the entry. 'How come you're here when you're on television? Are you really Dr Gareth Gordon? Gran says you're a twin.'

Marnie heard the jumble of words and wondered if she could disappear beneath the wrapping paper. Then she heard Richard speaking again.

'I taped my bit of the show yesterday,' he explained, 'then did some business and flew back to spend Christmas with you lot. There's something extra in the car for you. You can go and get it out, providing you promise to stay outside for fifteen minutes.'

Marnie lifted her head to see what was going on.

He had his arms around all four children, but his eyes were on Jill.

'You time them, Jill. OK?'

Marnie saw her nod, then Richard released them and they dashed out the door.

'I'll put the kettle on,' her mother said and scurried off, leaving Marnie to face him alone.

'It is you? You are him?' she stuttered, feeling helpless and inadequate and utterly lost.

'It is me, and I am him,' he said, kneeling down in front of her and reaching out to take her hands. 'I should have told you, but I'd always prized my anonymity.

In fact, I'd refused to do the segment until that night with Jill. . .'

'You gave away your secret because of Jill?' Marnie asked as hope began to stir inside her.

'Because of Jill—and Kyle and all the children you and I don't know.'

He hesitated and she looked into his eyes and saw his concern.

'And because of you, who showed me so many manifestations of love that I was swept into territory I'd never entered before. It frightened me, Marnie, because I no longer felt in control of things, but even worse than that was the fear that I might hurt you and your little family.'

'Pete told me not to be afraid of my feelings,' she whispered, and Richard brushed his lips across her forehead.

'I wish he'd told me that,' he murmured. 'I've been terrified.'

'But you came back,' she pointed out. 'You're here for Christmas.'

'Isn't that where fathers should be?' he asked, and kissed her on the lips.

'Fathers?'

The word faltered from her lips.

'Well, father, singular—if they, and you, will have me.'

'But your work. . .your writing. . .?'

She stared at him, too overwhelmed by her own emotion to comprehend what he was saying.

'I came here to write,' he reminded her, kissing the tip of her nose. 'It's something I can do anywhere. And as for work, I've booked myself in for a general practice refresher course—'

'You'll work here? Work with Dr Crail? But he'll retire and you'll have no time to write.'

He silenced her with a kiss that found her lips.

'Will you stop worrying about my future and reply to my proposal?' The words were so softly spoken that she barely heard them. 'I have fixed it all—for you, and this community you love so much, and solved a few other people's problems along the way. You're not the only miracle-worker, my dearest love!'

Marnie wanted to ask how and why and a thousand other questions, but his final words, 'my dearest love', had made her mind go blank. Fortunately he continued to explain, holding her close and whispering the words into her ear.

'I've a medical acquaintance who writes mystery novels. We met through our publisher, and have often commiserated with each other about juggling "real" work and writing—'

'But your writing is real work,' she protested automatically, and was rewarded with a hug.

'Real enough to me,' Richard admitted. 'Anyway, it seems he'd decided to shift out of the city. His wife's also a GP, and they were thinking about a quiet country practice.'

Marnie moved away from him, turning so that she could see his face.

'You've found us a doctor? Two doctors?'

He smiled a smile that made her heart wobble.

'Three, if you count me,' he told her. 'Between the lot of us we should be able to take over from Dr Crail and have time to spare for other pursuits.'

His voice deepened and the look in his eyes made her blush.

'What do you think?' he asked, his voice husky with emotion.

She shook her head and pressed her hands against her flaming cheeks, but before she could reply Margaret had burst into the room.

'Kyle says we should call him Gareth but I think Alice is better.'

'Sure you want a family?' Marnie asked, hoping Richard could see the love she felt for him glowing in her eyes.

'Alice is a girl's name, silly, and he's a boy,' Mikey argued, following his sister into the room.

Then the 'present' appeared, a floppy-eared spaniel who spied the paper and dived into the mess with sharp barks of delight. Jill dived after it, trying to save the ribbons and bows.

'I tried to keep them outside longer,' Kyle said, smiling shyly as he looked from one adult to the other.

'It was long enough,' Richard told him, with a man-to-man grin that made Kyle blush. 'For the moment!' he added, and turned so he could put his arm around Marnie's shoulders.

'Well, Kyle thinks it's all sorted out so you'll have to marry me,' he whispered in her ear. 'I think we'll let it dawn gradually on the others. I'd hate to make some big announcement and find that Margaret disapproved.'

Marnie relaxed against his chest and kicked gently at the puppy who'd discovered her toes. Christmas carols from the television programme echoed around the room and the screen showed snowy fields and gabled houses. But nowhere, she decided, could Christmas be better than it was right here.

MILLS & BOON®

Medical Romance™

COMING NEXT MONTH

TO HAVE AND TO HOLD by Laura MacDonald

Book 1 Matchmaker Quartet

Georgina and Andrew had been married, now they were divorced. But their friend Helen knew it would only take a little gentle persuasion to get them back together again.

―――――――――∿―――――――――

THIRD TIME LUCKY by Josie Metcalfe

Final book St Augustine's *trilogy*

Hannah had her own reasons for not wanting a relationship. but when she finally sees Leo as more than a colleague, she finds it impossible *not* to get involved.

―――――――――∿―――――――――

HEALING THE BREAK by Patricia Robertson

The whole hospital believed Heather and Scott were a hot item. To stop the gossip, they decided to act—they would pretend to date and then end the relationship. Simple—or was it?

―――――――――∿―――――――――

A SURGEON'S SEARCH by Helen Shelton

Tessa wanted to say yes to James, but she knew she should say no—after all, James was her best friend. He couldn't be serious about wanting more, could he?

Available from WH Smith, John Menzies, Volume One, Forbuoys, Martins, Tesco, Asda and other paperback stockists.

WINTER WARMERS

How would you like to win a year's supply of Mills & Boon® books? Well you can and they're FREE! Simply complete the competition below and send it to us by 30th June 1998. The first five correct entries picked after the closing date will each win a year's subscription to the Mills & Boon series of their choice. What could be easier?

THERMAL SOCKS	RAINCOAT	RADIATOR
TIGHTS	WOOLY HAT	CARDIGAN
BLANKET	SCARF	LOG FIRE
WELLINGTONS	GLOVES	JUMPER

T	H	E	R	M	A	L	S	O	C	K	S
I	Q	S	R	E	P	M	U	J	I	N	O
G	A	S	T	I	S	N	O	I	O	E	E
H	T	G	R	A	D	I	A	T	O	R	L
T	A	C	A	R	D	I	G	A	N	A	T
S	H	F	G	O	L	N	Q	S	W	I	E
J	Y	H	J	K	I	Y	R	C	A	N	K
H	L	F	N	L	W	E	T	A	N	C	N
B	O	V	L	O	G	F	I	R	E	O	A
D	O	E	A	D	F	G	J	F	K	A	L
C	W	A	E	G	L	O	V	E	S	T	B

C7L

Please turn over for details of how to enter ⇨

HOW TO ENTER

There is a list of twelve items overleaf all of which are used to keep you warm and dry when it's cold and wet. Each of these items, is hidden somewhere in the grid for you to find. They may appear forwards, backwards or diagonally. As you find each one, draw a line through it. When you have found all twelve, don't forget to fill in the coupon below, pop this page into an envelope and post it today—you don't even need a stamp! Hurry competition ends 30th June 1998.

Mills & Boon Winter Warmers Competition
FREEPOST CN81, Croydon, Surrey, CR9 3WZ

EIRE readers send competition to PO Box 4546, Dublin 24.

Please tick the series you would like to receive
if you are one of the lucky winners

Presents™ ❏ Enchanted™ ❏ Medical Romance™ ❏
Historical Romance™ ❏ Temptation® ❏

Are you a Reader Service™ Subscriber?   Yes ❏   No ❏

Mrs/Ms/Miss/Mr.......................Initials ....
(BLOCK CAPITALS PLEASE)

Surname ....

Address ....

....

....Postcode ....

(I am over 18 years of age)   C7L

One application per household. Competition open to residents of the UK and Ireland only. You may be mailed with offers from other reputable companies as a result of this application. If you would prefer not to receive such offers, please tick box.   ❏

Mills & Boon® is a registered trademark of
Harlequin Mills & Boon Limited.